THE FALCON

CLAN ROSS OF SKYE

USA TODAY BESTSELLING AUTHOR

HILDIE MCQUEEN

STORIES THAT BRING THE MAGIC
OF SCOTLAND TO LIFE

The Falcon: Clan Ross of Skye
USA Today Bestselling **Author**
Hildie McQueen

Copyright © 2024 by Hildie McQueen
Print Edition

ISBN: 978-1-960608-08-6

ALSO BY HILDIE MCQUEEN

PROLOGUE

"D̲O YE FIND me bonny?" The lass gave Knox's ear a playful nip, her heated breath fanning over it.

"Of course I do. Why else would I be here?" He'd tupped the lass before. She was without complications, never demanding anything from him. Knox found it best not to ponder too much on why she didn't seem to mind that he didn't call on her regularly.

"What makes ye think I will give ye what ye want?" She leaned back to meet his gaze, her eyes twinkling with mischief.

Knox smiled. "I dinnae ken for sure. Ye may nae."

Just as he was about to kiss her, the unmistakable sound of footfalls, something or someone approaching got his attention. Unfazed, the lass leaned forward, eyes closed, with expectation, and for a moment Knox considered ignoring what he'd heard.

The cracking of a breaking branch sounded closer.

As a leader of the laird's guard, it would be disgraceful to be caught or attacked whilst under a woman's skirts. He'd never heard the end of it, especially if whoever approached was another guard.

"Wait here," he whispered. "If ye hear fighting run home."

Wide-eyed, her mouth formed an "O", and she nodded.

Despite the fact it could be no more than a deer or someone out for a leisurely walk, there had been attacks in the surrounding areas and he would always take the greatest care to ensure a woman's safety.

From the way the woman stood wringing her hands, any romantic notions were over. He motioned for the lass to leave. Best be safe.

Obviously frightened, the lass gave him one last longing look before lifting her skirts and dashing away.

With practiced steps from his many years as a guard and tracker, Knox crept in the direction of the sound making sure to step evenly and avoid branches that would crack under his weight. There was no one in sight. He scanned the surroundings and then studied the ground taking advantage of his expert tracking abilities.

A broken branch, a telltale sign of someone walking nearby, caught his attention. Interestingly, whatever direction the person or beast went was hard to tell until he noted the way leaves on one bush were brushed. Whoever or whatever it was had gone away from where he was.

Looking around the surroundings, he thought to have caught movement.

Sure it was a person, he moved behind a tree and slowly peered around the side. A branch flew across the air, he avoided the hit, and it crunched against the tree's bark instead.

Just as Knox was going to announce who he was, the branch swung again, its wielder letting out a loud screech. This time he jumped back to keep from being struck.

Slender and small in stature, the branch-wielding woman was no match for Knox's bulk and strength.

Whatever was the fiery lass thinking? He waited for the

next swing, grabbed the branch, and gave it a strong tug. The woman stumbled forward landing on all fours on the forest floor.

"Are ye daft?" he yelled, yanking the woman up by an arm. "What are ye doing in the woods alone, Sencha?"

She looked a proper mess, skirts torn, and half her flame-red hair had loosened from its pins and spilled over her face.

Somehow, even in the disheveled state, she remained beautiful.

"Let me go!" She tried to pull away, whilst sweeping hair away from her flushed face. Her chest lifted and lowered as harsh breaths exploded.

When she tried to kick him, Knox easily avoided her attempts and glared at her. "Will ye stop acting like a wildling."

This time Knox grabbed her around the waist and pulled her close, making it harder for her to kick.

Pushing against his chest, she looked up and realized who he was and let out a huff. "What are ye doing here?"

She smelled of lavender and nature, her delicate figure fit perfectly between his arms and Knox was reluctant to release her.

"I will let ye go if ye promise not to try to hit me again." He purposely held her tighter, not as a warning, but because he'd always wondered what it would feel like to have the fiery lass in his arms.

"I thought ye were one of the attackers and meant to kill me," she replied breathlessly.

After one last inhalation of her hair, Knox released her.

"Knox, I didnae ken it was ye. Are ye here alone? I thought to have heard several voices." Her eyes darted in the direction of where he and the lass from the village had just been.

The way she tilted her heart-shaped face, as she studied him, made him want to lie. He glanced over his shoulder to the area where he'd been noting no one was about.

"I am alone," he replied, not a lie, per se. "And ye, what are ye doing?"

"Looking for Blossom, my wee dog. She ran off earlier." A crease formed between her brows. "I am quite worried."

He studied her torn skirts and messy hair. Apparently he wasn't the only obstacle in her search. "Ye seem to have had a time of it."

Eyes flattening, she looked down at her dress. "It is nae easy to traipse about the woods in skirts. Branches reach out and snag everything, my hair, my clothes, my skin." Sencha held out both arms to prove her point. Indeed they were covered with a few cuts and scratches.

In his opinion, women as beautiful as Sencha should never be so far from home without an escort. Even before the attacks, there was always the chance she'd run into men who had no scruples. Especially when they came across a fetching lass alone.

"Dogs are smart and return home when hungry. I doubt yer wee dog would venture so far away from where it is guaranteed food and shelter."

Sencha didn't look convinced, a frown on her features, she looked away from him, seeming to consider whether or not to continue her search. Then she studied him. "I am surprised ye are nae in the village chasing after women. Where's yer horse?"

"I am returning to the keep from patrolling and seeing

after the old MacKerns. Ye ken they live near here." He pointed to the right. "My steed is there."

Her eyes narrowed in thought, looking from the horse to him. "Why is yer horse tethered over there and ye are walking about the woods?"

The lass was smart. He had to acknowledge that a man involved with her would have to be someone who was either quick on his feet or honest at all times.

"I walked into the woods to find relief, when I heard ye step on a branch." Again not a lie, per se.

"Oh,"—her cheeks pinkened—"I see." She made shooing motions with her hands. "Well go on then. I will look a bit more for Blossom and then go home."

Now he had to pretend to relieve himself. Knox let out a breath. "I will walk ye home. Ye should nae be about on yer own. Even with the branch, which ye did wield well, harm can come to ye."

Knox held up a hand. "Wait here."

For a brief moment, he glanced toward the village thinking about the lass he'd been with. Perhaps he'd visit her and set her mind at ease the next time he visited his parents.

Knox went to where his horse was nibbling on the grass oblivious to what all had occurred and taking the reins he brought the huge warhorse to where Sencha waited.

IT WAS THE first time he'd had the opportunity to spend time alone with the pretty lass. Sencha was one of the few women who seemed immune to his charms. Although always friendly, she'd never seemed to consider him more than a childhood friend, an acquaintance.

That he knew of, no one had yet to court the flame-haired beauty. Not for lack of trying, but because she refused every man who attempted to court her.

"We have known each other for a long time," Knox said by way of conversation as they began walking side-by-side. It was time to try a new tactic, perhaps a closer friendship could lead to more.

"Aye, since we were wee," she replied giving him a sideways glance. "Ye are older, so we were never what I would consider friends."

His smile was careful, controlled. "Nothing stops us from being good friends now."

"I suppose."

"My heart melts by yer enthusiasm," he teased.

The words elicited a throaty laugh. "I dinnae mean to sound less than enthusiastic, it is that I am truly worried. My Blossom is wee and alone. What if a wild beast gets her?"

Knox whistled several times, whilst Sencha called out the dog's name. They continued in a wavy pattern heading back towards where Sencha lived. Knox was sure the dog was home by now, but he didn't wish to end the time spent with the lass just yet.

"Ye've had the dog for long?"

Sencha nodded. "Aye, over ten years, since she was pup. The runt of a litter, she was. Wee Blossom is getting old and cannae see well."

As they walked down the last patch of woods, Sencha looked as if about to cry. "Where can she be?" Her shiny eyes lifted to his. "Do ye really think she went home?"

It took all his willpower not to pull her close and comfort

her. Instead he acted as a friend would and placed a hand on her slight shoulder. "Let us go and find out. If she is nae at yer house, I will ride back and search for her."

"Thank ye, I do appreciate it." To his surprise, she threw her arms around his waist and hugged him. It wasn't a long hug and certainly not meant to be in any way flirtatious, but it made Knox feel as if he'd won first place in a competition.

Despite their continuous search while walking, the small dog was nowhere to be found.

A stately two-story stone house came to view, smoke emanating from the chimney promising warmth. The house was flanked by hills where cows and sheep grazed.

Thanks to Sencha's brother being a successful privateer sailing to and from the West Indies, they owned a large parcel of land. Her family was not extremely wealthy, but from what he'd heard, they were able to hire several farmhands and a pair of servants.

When they neared Sencha's house, a dog didnae trot out to greet them and Sencha let out a long sigh and once again looked to him. "It seems she is nae here."

"I will find her," Knox promised, unsure how to go about it since he had no idea what the dog looked like.

Just then the front door opened and an older woman, whom he recognized as Sencha's mother walked out. She wore a serviceable, but well-tailored dress.

"Sencha, where have ye been? I thought ye went for a walk in the garden," the woman called out as they neared.

Before Sencha could reply, her eyes narrowed at Knox and then took in the state of Sencha's clothes and hair. "Did something occur?"

Sencha let out a shaky breath. "I went searching for Blossom. I cannae find her. I came across Knox and he offered to help."

Shaking her head, her mother's gaze scanned from Sencha's disheveled hair to her torn skirts. "Lass, ye look a fright. Blossom returned a long while ago and is sleeping by the hearth. I was about to send someone out to search for *ye*."

"Oh," Sencha exclaimed, hands clutched over her chest. "I was so worried." She gave Knox an apologetic look. "Thank ye for helping me."

Her mother eyed Knox, seeming to see something. Perhaps his roguish reputation gave the woman pause.

Finally, she seemed to relax. "I am grateful she came upon ye. This foolish lass should nae have gone traipsing in the woods alone. Anything could happen, Sencha," she finished pinning her daughter with a look.

"Come in for some warm broth before ye continue on to wherever it is ye were heading," Sencha's mother added.

"I best not," Knox replied, not liking the way the woman watched him. It was as if she knew how strongly he was attracted to her daughter. "I am expected at the keep."

As he rode away, he glanced over his shoulder toward the house and a smile played on his lips. Perhaps he'd finally made headway towards getting to ken Sencha. Then, with a bit of patience, he would use all his well-honed skills to seduce the lass.

Seduce.

He waited for the excitement at the thought of the thrill of the hunt, but nothing happened. Instead the thought of seducing Sencha, for the sake of a tumble, felt wrong.

Something in his gut told him that if he ever accomplished this particular goal, there would be no going back. Sencha was not a one-time woman, but the kind of woman that bespelled a man to remain forever. For whatever reason, the idea of it didn't terrify him.

His decision changed. Perhaps it was best to stay away from her at all costs.

CHAPTER ONE

"**I** DINNAE REQUIRE more clothes at the moment," Sencha told her mother as they prepared to go to town.

Her mother looked her up and down. "Ye have nae had any new clothes in a pair of years and after tearing the skirt a few days ago, I realized it had been mended several times already."

Sencha had hoped to go to the Ross keep and visit her friend Nala for a few days. Instead, she was sure the trip to the village would take all day, and her mother planned for them to remain at least one night at her aunt and uncle's home.

"I'd hoped to go to the keep for a pair of days," Sencha began whilst braiding her hair. "I have nae seen Nala in almost a sennight."

"It will have to wait." Her mother left no room for argument and Sencha released a breath of resignation.

In truth, she'd not had a new dress made in a long time, but there was little that she required nice clothing for. She rarely attended any gatherings and the only people she and her mother visited were her aunt Jane and uncle Donald in the village and Nala and her parents at the keep.

In her estimation, her wardrobe of four skirts and just as many blouses and vests were enough for life on the isle. Granted two of her skirts had been repeatedly mended as she wore them while gardening, riding, or doing housework. The other pair were in better condition, and she could wear them to any obligatory function.

There was a knock on the door and her mother opened it to the farmhand, Gordon, who was to drive their carriage to the village. The bearded man was of good stature and had a very mild, gentle manner and had worked for them for many years.

"The carriage is ready," he announced, winking at Sencha.

She smiled back at him. "I just need to retrieve my bag." Dashing from the room, she noted her mother's flushed face. Sencha wanted to laugh. It had been obvious to her that both Gordon and her mother were attracted to each other. Why neither acted on it was beyond her understanding.

Her mother had been widowed longer than Gordon had been working there and once Sencha married, she'd be alone. Perhaps she'd do something to get their relationship moving along at a faster rate than merely passing looks.

Once they were settled in the small carriage, they began what would be a long drive. Usually the trip took about three hours, which meant they'd be there midday. Sencha hoped they'd be able to get to the market before the vendors were out of the items she wanted to purchase.

Peering out the window, she recognized the spot where she and Knox had battled. She almost laughed out loud.

"Why are ye smiling as if ye saw something humorous?" her mother asked.

Sencha shook her head. "When I was searching for Blossom, I attacked Knox with a branch, where we just passed. I thought he was a stranger lurking about the woods."

"If anyone was lurking, it was ye," her mother replied. "I cannae believe ye were this far. The dog would nae have gone so far."

The dog had gone further once, but Sencha refrained from telling her mother. She'd be worried that Sencha had dared to go even farther after it.

"I suppose it would seem that I was lurking. Although I was calling out Blossom's name." She settled back in the seat. "What do ye plan to do at the village, Mother?"

"First stop will be the village square, then onto the seamstress. After, we will go to Jane's house," her mother replied, referring to her sister. "Is there anywhere ye would like to go?"

"I am hoping to find perfumed soap, oil, and some ribbons. I would also like to purchase Nala a gift. Perhaps, the basket weaver is there. He makes beautiful baskets."

"Aye, he does," her mother replied suddenly becoming animated. "I may purchase one as well. I need a gift for yer cousin Maura's wedding."

Seeing an opening, Sencha schooled her expression to hopefully seem as if the thought had suddenly come to her. "I think ye and Gordon would be a good couple. Ye should consider marriage, Mother."

Wide-eyed, her mother's mouth fell open. "Wh-why would that occur to ye?"

"Because he is a handsome man, and it is obvious he admires ye."

A light pink blush appeared on her mother's cheeks and Sencha's heart warmed. "Mother, when I marry, if it ever comes to be, I dinnae wish for ye to be alone." Before her mother could say anything, she quickly added, "Even if I am never to marry, ye are young and should have a husband."

"Athol will return and in all probability bring a wife with him. I would nae be alone," her mother replied.

"My brother is enamored with the sea and filling his coffers. I dinnae expect he will settle until he is unable to sail," Sencha said referring to her brother's obsession with sailing between Scotland and the West Indies.

"True," her mother agreed. "That son of mine would have a hard time away from the sea. However, we are on an isle and very close to water, so I'm sure he would be fine."

UPON ARRIVING AT the village, Gordon helped them out near the village square. From there they made their way to the small stands. While her mother lingered with a woman selling embroidered items, Sencha walked to the basket weaver's stand.

Across the square, at another stall, there was no mistaking the tall broad-shouldered man who stood talking to a woman. It was Knox.

Sencha knew the village girl, she was called Anni. She was pretty and quite flirtatious, with long dark hair and a curvy figure. At the moment as she stood talking to Knox, she switched from twirling her hair around a finger to tapping his arm playfully.

Sencha's eyes narrowed and she let out a soft huff. How did men fall for such obvious ploys for attention? If Knox wanted to be with a woman who was overtly flirtatious then good for him. In her opinion, it meant he was a shallow man.

Catching herself, she shook her head and let out a breath. At her nearing the basket weaver's stand, the seller's expression brightened, his smile wide, the gaps between his teeth at full display. "Miss Sencha. I have nae seen ye in more than a fortnight at least."

Unable to keep from it, Sencha grinned. "I have been here, but have avoided ye, so I can keep some coin." Her attention was instantly taken by his offerings. The lines of beautifully woven baskets made it hard to choose just one. Picking up one and then another, Sencha inspected each one with care.

"How are ye, Sencha?" Knox had neared without her noticing.

Ensuring to keep her attention on the basket despite the subtle skip of her heart, Sencha replied in what she hoped was an even tone. "I am well, Knox. Here with Mother to do a bit of shopping."

"That one is quite nice," Knox said looking at the basket in her hands.

"Aye, it is." Sencha looked at him.

With the shadowing of his beard along his jawline, his wind-tussled hair, a slight lift to his lips, *and* he had his tunic opened at the neck, he looked every bit a devilish rogue. A very, very handsome rogue at that.

Her mouth went dry, and she quickly turned her attention back to the basket weaver. "I would like this one please." The man's face fell just a bit, disappointed as she usually purchased at least two, but did his best to hide it and nodded. "Aye, of course." He quoted a price, expecting Sencha to haggle.

She gave him the full amount he asked making him brighten again. "I will insist Mother purchase one as well," Sencha said as her mother walked up.

It was always entertaining to see any interaction between

her mother and Knox, as he always seemed tongue-tied when in her presence. Sencha figured it was because, unlike most older women, her mother was not affected by his roguish charms.

"Knox, do ye nae have tasks to be performing for the laird?" her mother asked whilst giving him a pointed look.

"Aye Missus MacTavish. I am here waiting for..." He looked away seeming to search for something. With a look of relief, Knox motioned to the road where a group of guards on horseback appeared. "I best go see what happens.

He gave Sencha one last look and with a slight nod he hurried toward the guards.

WHILE HER MOTHER inspected the baskets, Sencha watched Knox's interaction with the guards. After a moment, he turned in her direction, with an unreadable expression. She couldn't tell if he was angry or worried. Surely it was her imagination, whatever they spoke of didn't have anything to do with her.

With their purchases in hand, Sencha and her mother left the market at the village square and went to the carriage to deposit them. Gordon placed the items into the back and promised to watch over things while they went to the seamstress's shop.

Just then, there was a commotion, and a group of guards reappeared. Walking in front of them was Knox, who seemed to be searching the gathering crowd.

"What happens?" her mother asked a young lad who scurried toward them.

The dirty faced boy hesitated and looked up to her, excited to have news to share. "They got Donald McMurray. Say he killed a fisherman." The boy ran off without waiting for another question.

The ground seemed to sway, but Sencha couldn't allow herself to fall because her mother had paled and looked about to faint.

"We must find my sister," her mother grabbed Sencha's hand and dragged her toward the guards.

Just then the guards neared, two of them holding her uncle Donald's arms. She and her mother didn't have to go any farther to find her aunt Jane. She was running behind them, grabbing at their tunics demanding them to let her husband go.

Before Sencha could stop her mother, she rushed into the fray, joining her sister, tugging at the two guard's tunics.

Obviously afraid they could be pushed away or harmed, Gordon appeared and with astounding strength grabbed both her mother and aunt around the waist and pulled them away.

He neared with the still struggling women, and he motioned with his head to the carriage. "Hurry, we must go to. They will take him to the keep."

Somehow between Sencha and Gordon they managed to get the two unconsolable women into the carriage.

"Sencha." Knox appeared behind her just as she was about to climb into the carriage. "I will ensure yer uncle is nae harmed. He will ride with me."

"Th-thank ye," Sencha managed, her voice cracking. "I dinnae understand what happens."

He looked past her into the carriage before meeting her gaze. "I dinnae either."

THE CARRIAGE ROCKED side to side as they rode over the uneven terrain to the Ross keep. After asking each other question after question—none of them truly understanding what had occurred—Sencha, her aunt, and her mother lapsed into a tense silence.

Her aunt had explained that the guards had arrived and taken her uncle without any explanation. After demanding an answer several times, one of them had said he'd been accused of killing a fisherman by the name of Fitz. That was all she knew.

Sniffing broke the silence as they rode through the gates into the keep's courtyard. All three leaned forward and peered out to try and catch a glimpse of her uncle, but neither he nor the guards were in sight.

Finally, they came to a stop and Gordon opened the door, helping them out one by one onto the cobbled surface. All three rushed to the front door of the main hall, hoping to find out that it had all been a huge mistake. After all, her uncle was the gentlest, kindest man she'd ever known. How anyone could possibly think he would kill anyone was beyond belief.

The great room was full of activity. People sat at tables. Others lined up waiting for their turn to seek an audience with the laird. A few lingered, seeming to not have any reason for being there. Perhaps they stayed in hopes of a good meal.

Her uncle stood between two large warriors, his head up, shoulders straight as he faced Laird Alexander Ross.

Knox was also there, standing to the side. With all the chatter and activity, it was hard to hear what was being said from the back of the room. The situation was quickly remedied when her aunt and mother pushed their way through those gathered at the front. Sencha, feeling she had no other option but to follow, hurried to catch up.

If the laird found their intrusion unacceptable, he didn't show it. Instead he kept his attention on what was being read by the man who sat at a small table with quill in hand.

The scribe glanced up then again began reading from the parchment he held. "There was a witness that saw Donald McMurray walking to Fitz's cottage with a knife in his hand. Another witness saw the same man hurrying away back toward town. Not long later, Fitz was found dead, a knife just like the one McMurray was seen carrying impaled in his chest."

There were gasps from those who had heard, including her mother. Her aunt swayed but managed to stay upright.

"My husband didnae kill anyone. He would never!" she yelled.

The laird turned to her aunt and a guard came to stand next to her, the message clear. If she dared to speak up again, she would be removed.

"What do ye have to say?" the laird asked, his voice calm and clear. Of course, he probably heard things like this regularly.

As her uncle explained he had indeed gone to the fishing huts, he didnae seek out the man called Fitz, but another fisherman whom he'd borrowed the knife from. The man he sought had already gone out fishing, so he'd left the knife in the man's hut.

There were murmurs as the laird contemplated the explanation.

"Ye will remain here at the keep, under lock and key, until this matter is cleared. People will be questioned tomorrow, and I will hear what everyone has to say. At that time, I will decide if ye will be held responsible or nae. If ye are, ye will be hung."

This time it was her uncle who swayed while her aunt fell into a dead faint.

CHAPTER TWO

"WE MUST SPEAK to my uncle." Sencha grabbed Knox's arm, with a hold tight. "Please, allow us to care for his wounds. It seems he must have fallen because he's blending from both knees."

It was true. Before he'd been able to get to the man, the guards had already bound him, and he'd fallen before reaching the horses.

"It is just scrapes. He is nae injured. Ye cannae see him yet," he replied knowing it wasn't at all what Sencha wanted to hear.

Her grip became tighter. "Please."

Just then, both her aunt and mother hurried over to join them. The three sets of pleading eyes bored into him.

Making matters worse, Nala Ross, Alexander's wife and Sencha's closest friend came running through the great room and threw her arms around Sencha. "I just heard. I am so sorry."

To his horror, Sencha began to cry. Tears streamed down her pretty face, and the tip of her nose turned red.

Knox wanted to hurry away, there was nothing worse than a woman crying, especially one he found beautiful. He swallowed and shifted his feet trying to decide what to do.

"Knox." Nala's dark brown eyes narrowed at him. "Why

can they nae see him?"

"Alex will nae allow it until after he is questioned. It may be a long wait."

When his aunt—the woman who'd raised him like her own—appeared, he wanted to sag in relief.

She gave him an understanding look. Many times this scenario had played out and she always helped with the women who were affected. Nala was newly married, but Knox was sure she'd learn in time to do the same, to help in a way that put the family at ease without interfering with what had to be done.

"Come, let us go into the sitting room and have something strong to drink while we wait." His aunt held out her arms ushering them through to the other side of the great room and out to a room that was surrounded by windows that let in sunlight, with plenty of comfortable seating.

It wasn't until the last skirt disappeared from sight that Knox let out a breath. The next days would be hard for the accused man's family.

One thing he was certain about, Donald McMurray was not a killer. He'd a chance to talk to the man on the way to the keep. Other than being baffled and confused, the man was terrified of what occurred. Never once did he waver in his story of what had happened the day before. And after many years as a warrior, one thing Knox had finessed—other than his archery—was knowing when a man lied.

However, it was one thing knowing the truth, another thing altogether was proving it.

He stalked to the small room where Donald McMurray had been taken. Two guards kept vigil outside while Cynden

Ross, the laird's youngest brother, and a pair of council members were already inside.

Standing before the seated men, the confused bedraggled Donald ran his hands through his sparse hair making it stand on end as he looked about the room with obvious fear.

"I swear it. I never went to Fitz's hut. I went to return a knife to another fisherman, then left promptly." As he spoke his eyes darted about the small room making eye contact, not wavering other than to swallow visibly.

"I believe him," Knox said from the doorway. When the men inside turned to him, words left him. Other than gut instinct, he had no way to prove the man's innocence.

"Whether we believe him or not, there are witnesses to the fact that he went in the direction of the dead man's home and returned with haste from the same," one of the councilmen stated.

"Do ye have anything else to say?" Cynden asked Donald who shook his head.

"Ye will remain here until it is time for Alexander to decide yer fate," the other councilmen said. "Sustenance will be brought to ye."

With that, they walked out. Cynden looked at Knox. "I also believe he may be innocent. We will speak to the witness who came forth and then perhaps go to the village and see if others can be found."

They went to an adjacent room, where the witness waited. The lanky older man seemed nervous, but unlike Donald, he would be leaving and returning home that day.

The man was questioned, and he confirmed seeing Donald returning from near the dead man's hut, seeming frazzled.

When more questions were asked, it became clear that the hut of the fisherman Donald claimed to have gone to, would have made him come from another direction.

Either the witness lied, or the accused man did.

THE DAY WAS coming to an end, so Knox went to the great room to wait for last meal and assist where he could in dealing with those there to have matters settled by the laird.

By the time most of the people had gone, his stomach was constantly growling. Thankfully, kitchen lads hurried out with buckets of hot water and cloths and wiped the tabletops. Just after maids emerged carrying baskets of bread and platters containing meat and vegetables.

As the last meal began, the women emerged from the parlor. Sencha, her mother, and her aunt all had somber expressions as they were guided to sit at a table with the Ross women.

Knox was sure they'd barely taste the food, if they ate at all. He felt bad for Donald's wife, the poor woman's eyes were swollen from crying.

Sencha seemed angrier than sad, her eyes darting about the room. Just as the other women began to eat, she rose with a plate full of food. He knew what she planned and pushed back from the table.

Placing a hand on her shoulder, he stopped Sencha from going further away from her table. "Yer uncle received the same meal. There is nae need for ye to give up yer food."

"Can I eat with him then?" Her eyes snapped to his. "Or will he be forced to eat alone?"

He lowered his voice in hopes her aunt wouldn't hear.

"Until he is cleared, he is a prisoner. Like ye, I dinnae care for the situation. Dinnae make it harder for him or yer aunt by asking for privileges that will nae be granted."

For a moment he thought she'd retort. Instead, she turned away and lowered to sit. The other women around the table were silent as Sencha settled.

"Uncle Donald is having the same meal," she relayed to the group. "There is nae need for me to bring him food. That is good to hear is it nae, Aunt?"

The sad woman nodded. "Aye, I am glad he is going to eat well." Her reddened gaze lifted to Knox.

"He will have more than his fill, I assure ye," Knox said.

"What was that about?" Alex asked when he lowered to sit next to his cousin.

"They are worried about the prisoner's meal. I assured them, he ate the same as us." Knox glanced in Sencha's direction. "She is yer wife's close friend. It will make things difficult."

Alex shook his head. "Aye, I have had an earful from Nala already about the situation. We must find the truth immediately or I fear my wife will make me sleep in another room."

"I will go to the village and fishermen's area first thing in the morning. Can ye put off sentencing for at least one additional day?"

The dead man's sister and her husband were there demanding justice. Fitz had been unmarried and had lived a quiet life. However not having a wife didn't mean rules would be changed. Any kind of leniency toward Donald would look unfavorable for Alex.

"The two days stand until sunset. Unless otherwise proven

innocent, he will hang."

"We have only a man seeing walking from the direction of the huts." Knox couldn't keep the exasperation from his voice. "Ye cannae hang a man over that."

"He went with a knife and returned without it. The knife was nae found at the man's hut where he claimed to leave it."

"The fisherman was gone; anyone could have come in and taken it."

Alex let out a breath. "I ken, cousin. Go and find out the truth."

Knox understood the dilemma, but there was only so much that could be accomplished in just one day. The fishermen would sometimes be gone out to sea for more than a pair of days. If someone had seen something and gone fishing unaware of what they had witnessed, there was little that could be done until they returned. If the fisherman to whom the knife belonged had come in, taken the knife back out with him, and would not return for more than two days, then it could be Donald's fate was sealed.

"I will go now then," Knox said standing. "It is not far to the village; the fishermen should be back from their day."

He walked to the table where guardsmen sat and motioned to two men who were his closest friends: Hendry and Liam. "I must go to the fishermen's huts. Come with me."

Neither man hesitated. Both stood and followed him from the room. Liam clutched a tankard of ale and Hendry a chuck of bread topped with meat. What they'd grabbed said a lot about their personality.

HIS COMPANIONS RARELY questioned the reason why they

required each other's presence as trust in one another was firm. This time it was no different, neither seeming to mind riding in silence until past the gates.

Obviously he must have had a murderous expression because both looked to him and then exchanged glances.

Finally Hendry spoke. "Are we there to question people or beat them to death?"

Liam barked out a laugh. "By Knox's expression—both."

"I am nae happy to have my last meal interrupted. I am still hungry." Knox supposed he wasn't happy with the situation at all. Justice in the Highlands was swift and almost always fair. However, there were times like this that he hated the lack of a thorough inquiry into a crime before the accused were found either innocent or guilty.

The sun setting on the water gave it a magical effect, the soft waves seeming to be alive as the light played over them. Salty air blew across to the riders with a combination of moisture and chilliness.

As expected upon reaching the shoreline near the fishing huts, most of the fishermen were returning from a day out. Some sold fish, while others untangled nets and washed out their boats in preparation for the following morning. By their rounded backs, most were weary and ready to go home to eat and rest. They were hardworking men eking out a living from their daily toils.

Knox and his men dismounted and while Hendry and Liam went to speak to others, he made a beeline for one who'd eyed them nervously since noticing them.

"Do ye ken a man called Fitz?" Knox began as he neared the man.

The man tugged a net from his boat and shrugged. "A bit."

"This morning before leaving to fish, did ye see him?" Knox toed the net in the man's hands.

"He and another man were arguing when I walked past. I didnae get involved. But noticed he was nae out fishing today."

For someone who wasn't involved, the man gave a lot of information. "What is yer name?"

"I am called Kyle," the man replied placing his nets into the boat and lifting a bucket. He gave Knox a pensive look. "Would the laird be interested in fish?"

"Who was Fitz arguing with?" Knox asked ignoring the man's question.

The man shrugged looking around as if somehow the answer was among the other men there. "A man from the village. I believe he is called Donald."

Knox's stomach sank. "What did they argue about?"

This time the man seemed annoyed. "How am I to ken? I was just walking past."

The man started to walk away, but Knox stopped him. "Be at the keep first thing in the morning. Ye must speak to the council about this."

Kyle's eyes widened. "Why? I didnae see more than the argument."

"Because I insist." Knox met the man's gaze noting Kyle's eyes darting away, not meeting his. "If ye are nae there, I will send guards to fetch ye."

The pungent smell of rotted fish, which the fishermen used for bait, lingered as Knox made his way past a pair of boats to another man who still staring out at the water. When he neared, the man looked to him with a mournful expression.

"Is it true?" he asked. "Fitz is dead? Was killed?"

Knox nodded. "Aye, this morning. Stabbed to death."

The man visibly flinched. "Poor sod. I will miss 'im."

"Ye were friends then?"

By the man's sad smile, it was obvious he reminisced. "Of sorts. Had good banter most mornings and sometimes we fished near one another to keep each other company. Ye see, neither he nor I have close family." The man left the sentence hanging, seeming to be lost in thought once again.

"Did Fitz confide to ye about any feuds with anyone?" Knox studied the older man, his mourning so obvious it was tangible. "I understand ye. It is hard to lose a friend."

The man lifted his gaze to Knox, seeming to shrink, his shoulders sagging. "I am called Hugh. He slid a look in Kyle's direction. I dinnae ken anything about this morning. I went out earlier than usual as I wanted to return early to go to town. I am just now returning from town to prepare for tomorrow. It is where I heard about poor Fitz." Hugh's voice cracked as he finished.

Knox waited to allow the man to regain his composure.

Finally, Hugh continued, "Fitz was arguing with someone, perhaps two days past. I could nae hear but saw him and the other man shove each other. The man Fitz argued with had his back to me. I cannae tell ye who it was. I was too far out to see clearly. My eyesight is nae what it was. The only reason I knew one of the men was Fitz was because once he boarded his boat, he came near me as he passed."

"Can ye tell me at least if the man he spoke to was tall or short?" Knox prodded.

Hugh's brow creased. "Not short. The man he argued with

was taller than him."

After informing Hugh that he must come to the keep the following morning, Knox, Hendry and Liam decided to ride through the village on the way back.

"The only thing I found out was that Fitz kept to himself mostly," Hendry stated. "His only close friend was the man ye spoke to, Hugh."

"Aye, I gathered that," Knox replied. "He claimed to have seen Fitz having a heated discussion with a taller man two days prior. That will nae help much, but at least we ken he had another argument two days prior to his murder and the man was tall. So it could be it was the same person he argued with the day he was killed."

Hendry shook his head. "It is unfortunate that Kyle claims it was Donald who was with Fitz on the actual day."

They neared the tavern and Knox motioned to the others. "I must eat something. I am quite hungry."

THE TAVERN WAS a sharp contrast to the shoreline. Lanterns on multiple surfaces gave the interior a cheery feel. A fiddler sat atop a stool in one corner, playing a lively tune that seemed to entwine with the hum of conversations. There was a smoky haze from the fire in the hearth that added to the charm. The smell of burning wood mixed with the aroma of whatever was being cooked over the fire.

Finding a table just inside the door, Knox and his men sat and were promptly seen to by a buxom young lass whose gaze moved to each of them with a playful smile on her lips.

"What would the handsome gents wish for on this fine night?"

They ordered ales and Knox a bowl of stew.

The food was flavorful. Combined with the pretty woman who brought it along with delicious crusty bread, he was glad to have stopped.

When he stood to leave, he wandered over to speak to the barkeep.

"Oy, Angus. Have ye heard anything new about the killing?" Knox asked keeping a neutral expression.

The barkeep was in his forties, with bright red hair and beard. He'd inherited the tavern from his father and was well-liked.

He stroked the beard thoughtfully before replying. "Everyone's talking about it. Making things up as they go along. I didnae ken Fitz that well, he rarely stopped by. His cousin, Kyle, stops by a bit more. They never got along, so rarely were here at the same time."

Interesting that Kyle had not mentioned they were cousins and had even alluded to not knowing Fitz well. He'd have to ask the man more questions in the morning.

IT WAS EVENING by the time Knox, Liam, and Hendry returned to the keep. There was still activity in the great room as people had remained after the last meal. Some for the hearings the following day. Others out of curiosity to see what would happen to the prisoner.

In his study away from all the noise, Alexander waited to hear what they'd found out. As Knox, Hendry, and Liam described their conversations, the laird listened intently.

"It seems we have more questions than answers," Alexander said. "The morning will hopefully bring clarity." He didn't sound convinced.

Knox stood. "If nothing else is required, I will stop to see Donald and then go to find my bed." Leaving the office, he strolled through the great room, noting that Sencha and her relatives were not about. They'd probably gone to bed, planning to get up early and be present for whatever came next.

The short corridor to where Donald was kept was lit by a single sconce on the wall opposite the door. Knox waited for the guard to unlock it, and he stepped inside.

Seeming to have shrunk from his already small size, the older man sat in a chair by a small window. He looked up at Knox with hopeful eyes. "Any news?"

Knox sat on one of the other chairs and stretched. He was weary to his bones. "Do ye ken a mall called Kyle?"

Donald frowned and after a moment shook his head. "I do, but not well. He is another fisherman."

"He claims to have seen ye and Fitz arguing this morning."

"Then he lies," Donald stated emphatically. "I never saw or spoke to Fitz this morning. I saw no one at the fishing huts. Even when I looked to the shoreline, most of the boats were already gone."

The man let out a weary sigh. "I told all this to his laird-ship's brother this morning. I only went to drop the knife off at a man called Guiles's hut. I'd hoped to catch him before he left so he would hold back fish for me and bring it by my house. Ye see, he goes out for two or three days at a time."

It was the same thing Donald had said since that morning, his story not changing, his stance not wavering.

Knox believed Sencha's uncle, but he had to find more

proof. Hopefully the next day would bring new possibilities.

As he neared the stairwell to head up to his bedchamber on the second floor, a woman leaned out from a vestibule behind the stairs and motioned to him.

It was Anni. The pretty village girl had come earlier that day with her father, who wished to meet with Alexander.

"Knox," she whispered upon him walking up. "Ye look weary."

"I am," he admitted. "What are ye doing here?"

She bit her bottom lip and looked up at him with round eyes. "I saw ye walking toward the kitchens. Knowing ye'd returned, I came here in hopes of a private moment."

Her intent was obvious, and Knox wanted to groan in annoyance that he was much too tired to do more than stand.

Anni reached up and slid a finger down the side of his face, her gaze lingering on his lips.

Knox leaned forward. "I wish I could give ye some time, but I am quite tired tonight." Just as he was about to lean closer to press a kiss to her lips, a voice sounded from the stairs.

"Where did I leave my shawl," an exasperated Sencha whispered. Moments later, she appeared and hurried past toward the parlor not seeing them.

"I best go," Knox said and hurriedly pressed a chaste kiss to Anni's cheek. Before she could say anything more, he walked around to the stairs and up to the second floor.

"KNOX?" SENCHA CAUGHT up with him as he got to his bedchamber door.

He turned surprised to find her out and about. She'd

brushed her hair down and had wrapped her shawl around what looked to be her nightshift.

"Uh… aye?" He managed to drag his gaze to her face.

"Thank ye for all ye did today." It was dim in the corridor, but he could make out her face clearly. She looked on the brink of tears.

"There is nae need to thank me. I dinnae believe yer uncle killed that man, and I will do my best to prove it."

Pressing a hand to his chest, she closed her eyes and nodded. "We dinnae ken what would happen if ye didnae help us."

It was interesting that the simple touch was like a bolt of lightning, awareness traveling through his body. If not for sheer willpower, he would have covered her hand with his to keep her from moving it.

"The morning will bring clarity. It is what I hope," he said in a hoarse tone.

She managed a weak smile, pulling her hand away. Knox felt the absence immediately. "Sencha."

Tears threatened to spill from her beautiful eyes when they lifted to meet his. Then to his astonishment, Sencha threw herself against him, her arms around his middle, face shoved into the crook of his neck when he leaned forward to hug her back. "My uncle didnae do this. What will happen if he is hung? I cannae even think of it," her muffled words pierced him.

There was nothing he could say, instead he held her tightly wishing with all his might that there was a way to take her pain from her.

"Have faith, the truth will come out," Knox managed, unable to think of what else to say.

"I should allow ye to get some rest." Sencha moved away, her cheeks flushed, and the tip of her nose reddened.

Despite his weariness, he wanted to remain with her, holding her.

When she rounded him to walk past to where she shared a room with her mother and aunt, he turned to follow her progress.

CHAPTER THREE

L EAVING HER MOTHER and aunt sleeping, Sencha hurried from the bedchamber hoping to catch Knox and ask questions about what he'd discovered the day before.

If not for the fact he looked barely able to remain upright the night before, she would have asked that they discuss all that had occurred on his trip to the fishing huts. There was so much she was discovering about Knox. His caring way and the fact that he was the only one who fought for her uncle. Of course Alexander had to remain impartial, but he had to ken that her uncle would never do something like this.

Already, her aunt and mother had pleaded with him to see the truth and to be fair about the entire situation. According to her mother, he'd been understanding, but at the same time had explained he had to hear all sides before deciding. It was also the council who had to be convinced, as he and the council were to be united in what they considered to be the truth.

Despite the early hour, people who'd slept on the floor of the great room were rousing, and servants meandered about lighting lanterns and starting their tasks.

Sencha went to a young man who added wood to a stack by the hearth and inquired if he'd seen Knox. The young man informed her the guards met at that hour on the open field just outside the gates adding that Knox and the archers went to archery practice straight after.

Gazing toward the corridor that led to where her uncle was held, she considered asking to see him. But it was too early, and he probably still slept. Besides, it was best to speak to him once she had information to hopefully lift his spirits.

OUTSIDE THE MORNING air remained chilly, the skies above gray and cloudy. There was more activity in the courtyard. Servants carried pails from the well, horses were led from the stables, and men stood around a bonfire talking.

Making her way to the gates, she stood there looking toward the field where about twenty men stood. They formed a formidable sight, with either quivers and bows, or swords strapped to their battle-honed bodies. Each man wore a stoic expression as they listened to the men who stood before them.

Alexander, Cynden, and Knox stood before the men. It looked like it was Alexander who addressed the group. Probably giving instructions for the day and informing them of what to expect.

It would be a busy day for the men as there would be on-lookers coming to find out what would happen to her uncle. The thought of it made her eyes sting as she fought to keep from crying.

Her wonderful gentle uncle didn't deserve what happened. Every part of her being demanded that she fight to have him set free. And she would.

It wasn't a long wait before the guardsmen dispersed, some heading to the gate and walls, others to their sleeping quarters, and yet another group remained on the practice field. Knox was among those who remained.

Despite not wishing to approach while the laird and Cynden remained, Sencha needed to find out what she could. It wasn't that she was intimidated by his cousins, after all, they'd all grown up together. It was that she didn't want to give the impression that she demanded favoritism. Which of course she did.

Knox and his cousins all knew her uncle, they had to ken it was not in his nature to cause harm to another human being.

At seeing her, Knox headed toward her his shoulder-length hair blowing away from his face. The tiredness from the night before gone, he looked every bit an impressive warrior. His hazel gaze met hers and it was as if he touched her face. Sencha almost reached up to cup her own cheek.

The closer he got, the safer she felt. It was as if a warm cloak was placed over her shoulders.

"I need to speak with ye," Sencha asked meeting his gaze. "What did ye find out yesterday?"

Knox drew closer and took her elbow. "I can meet ye in the great room after I speak with the archers."

He looked across the courtyard where several men with bows in hand waited. "I will tell ye that Alexander will be speaking to two or three people who will come from the village later this morning. They are witnesses."

"Who are they? Will they speak against my uncle?"

He shook his head. "Both against and for." He gave her a pointed look. "I dinnae expect anything will be decided today." With that, he turned and walked back to where the archers waited.

It would not do to wait while other people helped decide

the fate of an innocent man. Sencha wanted to run after Knox and inform him that her uncle's fate was more important than stupid archery practice or whatever it was he did. Irritation filled her and she hurried back into the house and through the great room.

Upon reaching the short corridor to where her uncle was, the guard gave her a sharp command to stop.

"I must speak to my uncle." Sencha continued forward, not willing to be intimidated by a man she'd known since they were children. "Liam let me speak to him."

The guard blew out a breath. "Fine but be quick about it."

She gave him a droll look. "What does it matter? Ye are nae going anywhere anytime soon."

Other than a huff, he didn't reply. Instead, he turned and unlocked the door, opened it and peered in. Then motioned for her to enter leaving the door open.

Her uncle stood by the small window that gave him a view of nothing but the wall surrounding the keep.

"Sencha how are ye this morn?" He opened his arms, and she rushed to him fortifying against any tears.

They sat and he gave her a quizzical look. "What are ye doing up so early?"

"I want to ask ye a couple questions," she began. "What is the name of the man ye went to see to return the knife? Why did ye have the knife? Are ye sure to not have seen anyone when she went inside the hut to leave it?"

Her uncle rubbed both hands down his face, then stared blankly ahead. "The fisherman's name is Guiles. He and I met at the village square when he came to sell fish about a fortnight ago. When I got home, I realized I had his knife in the basket with the fish. I kept forgetting to return it. The other morning, yer aunt told me she had a craving to make fish stew. I told her I'd buy some from Guiles."

"So ye went to bring the knife and to meet with him?" Sencha asked.

"Aye," her uncle replied. "I thought that I could return it and find out when I might return to purchase some fish, I was told he is usually gone for two or three days."

Sencha tried to picture who the man was, but she couldn't recall anyone by the name Guiles, especially as she couldn't recall the last time she'd gone to the shore where the fishing huts were.

Her uncle continued, "I saw several people on my way there, greeting them as I went. On the way back, I stopped at the baker. If I had stabbed someone with a knife, surely there would have been blood upon my clothing."

The baker would have to come to testify, Sencha decided. "Anyone else ye spoke to upon yer return?"

"I remembered that I'd nae fed the chickens, so I left the baker and hurried home." Her uncle gave her a weak smile. "That is all I can tell ye about that day. The fishing huts seemed empty to me."

Sencha had an idea. "How did ye ken where the man called Guiles lived?"

"I didnae. I wandered about and asked a lad, he told me." His eyes brightened. "That's it, the young lad, he would ken where I went and what I did."

"What did he look like?" Sencha asked leaning forward with excitement. "Do ye recall anything about him?"

Scratching his head in thought, her uncle shook his head.

"Skinny, with a missing front tooth, looked to be about ten. Rather ragged, a street urchin, probably looking for things to steal."

"That's something," Sencha said. "Did ye tell the council about the boy?"

Her uncle shook his head. "I was so confused and scared. I forgot. But I will today."

"I best go." Sencha stood and pressed a hand on her uncle's shoulder. "This will be sorted. I promise."

She had to find Gordon and insist he take her to the fishing village. It was imperative to find the boy and bring him back to tell Alexander what all he'd seen the morning of the killing.

Hurrying back outside, she went out to the stables.

The smell of horses and hay was thick in the air as men guided the beasts outside while others cleaned the stables.

"Have ye seen Gordon, the man who brought my aunt, my mother, and me here?" she asked a young man, who'd she'd seen speaking to Gordon a day earlier.

The man studied her for a moment before recognition brightened his face. "Aye, he left earlier. Said he'd be back midday at the earliest."

Her spirit sank, eyes looking past him, hoping against hope Gordon was within sight. "Is there a horse I can ride? It is very important."

The young man shrugged. "I will ask."

Sencha hurried to the house to retrieve a cloak. Skirting quickly past the great room to avoid seeing her mother or aunt, she went up the stairs.

When she went back out, Sencha quickly mounted and

looked to the lad who worked at the stables. "Would ye please give a message to Knox Ross? Tell him that I have gone to the fishermen's huts."

The young man nodded, and she guided the mare through the courtyard and past the gates. Something had to be done, she had to find the lad who'd seen her uncle the day Fitz was killed.

IT WAS NOT a long way to the fishing village, unfortunately it had rained the night before, which left the road muddy, forcing the horse to a slower pace. It suited Sencha as she wasn't an experienced rider. Usually, Gordon took her anywhere she wished to go, whether to visit Nala or to the village. Other than that, she usually walked.

Upon nearing, the fishing village seemed empty, which made sense as it was still early. From the shoreline, several boats were visible in the distance. Atop gentle waves, the men stood in their vessels, tossing out nets or dragging them back in.

Sencha dismounted and with her hand across her brow she watched for a moment before turning toward the huts. A pack of dogs meandered, not seeming to find her interesting enough to pay any attention to. Instead, they sniffed the ground searching for something to eat.

In hopes of finding the boy her uncle had described, Sencha hurried past each hut, looking from left to right for any movement. It seemed no one was about. Not one single person lingered around the huts.

"Are ye looking for someone?" The raspy male's voice startled her, and Sencha whirled to find a tall lanky man leaning on the doorway of a hut she'd walked past.

He'd not been there just a moment earlier. Lips twisted into a snarl, he spat on the ground as he studied her. "Can ye nae talk?"

"I am looking for a young lad," Sencha replied, then tried to come up with a reason. "He…he stole something from me. I am told he spends time here."

The man took a step forward. "What did he steal?"

Sencha didn't like the man's expression, something about him made her skin crawl. Taking a step back, she looked around, angry she'd not thought to bring another person with her. "Have ye seen a lad of about ten about?"

The man's eyes narrowed. "Why are ye alone? Surely ye came without permission. Why are ye really here?"

"Never ye mind," Sencha snapped, doing her best to not show fear. "I came for what is mine. Nae to talk."

Her bravado must have worked because the man finally shrugged. "If the boy is around, he hides."

It occurred to Sencha that if the man was a fisherman, he'd not gone out. He was probably one of the witnesses. By his demeanor, she doubted he would do anything to help her uncle. Although there was no way to ken for sure and she wasn't about to ask.

It was best to leave and go to the village. There she could get the constable to help her find the boy. Sencha eyed the horse, wishing she could magically leap onto its back. "I will eventually find him."

Rounding the man, she could barely keep from running. In hindsight, running would have been a good idea because when she was but a couple of steps away from the man, something hard hit across the back of her head.

As the pain registered, Sencha landed face-first onto the ground. Everything blurred as she desperately tried to scramble away but she didn't make it far. A heavy foot pressed onto the center of her back. The weight increased flattening Sencha into the muddied earth.

Not only was it hard to breathe, but impossible to scream, not that anyone would hear her as all the fishermen had already left the shore in search of their catches for the day.

Fear and pain battled to be forerunners, the pounding of her heart not helping with the inability to breathe. Sencha desperately raked at the sandy dirt until finally able to turn her face sideways. Unfortunately because of the weight of the man's foot, it was hard to take more than shallow breaths.

Despite the terror she wanted to sag in relief when the man lifted his foot and yanked her up to stand, fingers digging painfully into her arms.

"I dinnae ken why yer here, but I do ken ye lie." His rancid bread filled her nostrils as she gasped air into her depleted lungs.

Realization struck. The man acted in such a way because it was probable he was the killer.

Sencha swallowed. "Let me go. My escort will be here shortly to search for me."

The man huffed obviously not believing her then half-dragged her forward.

Although raised to be gentle and feminine, she wasn't about to allow this man to take her without a fight. She kicked with as much strength as she could muster, satisfied when the man flinched and cursed. The result was his grip tightening around her upper arms, but she didn't stop struggling against the hold.

Lowering her head, she sunk her teeth into the man's right hand and he yelped in pain lessening his hold on her. Sencha attempted to escape, but his other hand remained firm on her arm. Sencha stopped on his foot, and he yowled in pain relinquishing his hold.

She barely made it a couple of steps before the man caught her by the arm, whirled her around, and plunged his fist into her stomach.

Letting out a loud "oof" all air left her body and Sencha stumbled backward barely able to keep from falling. Then the second hit came. This time his fist struck the side of her face, and she collapsed to the ground.

"Get up bitch," the man said through gritted teeth, yanking her up by the hair.

When he slapped her across the face, she lost the battle, and all went dark.

CHAPTER FOUR

T HE WELL WATER had a fresh earthy flavor as Knox drank deeply from it. He'd finished going over the assignments for the day with the archers. They'd be spread thin that day, several posted on every wall surrounding the keep and a couple atop the castle.

As for himself, he had to speak to Sencha, then once again to Donald. Already he'd explained to Alexander that he wished to return to the fishing area and the village one last time in hopes of gathering more information before the laird and council would decide Donald McMurray's fate.

There was a commotion, people running ahead and several others scurrying to see what was afoot as a coach, escorted by a group of mounted guards, rolled into the courtyard.

Alert to the possible threat, Knox raced to the side of the coach joining several other guards who did the same.

Heath MacTavish, a stout man who Knox recognized as a wealthy landowner climbed from the coach and looked to the other guards before zeroing in on him.

"I must speak to the laird immediately," he demanded, face turning red.

"I will escort ye in, but ye must calm. We dinnae allow someone who is a possible threat into the great room where our laird presides."

The man's nostrils flared, but he managed a curt nod. "I am no threat to Laird Ross." He motioned to the impressive lineup of guards.

"Yet ye bring an armed escort." Knox glanced to the mounted guards. "Why is that?"

MacTavish huffed indignantly. "Protection on the road. Enough of this. I must speak to Alexander Ross."

When the man managed to calm, he was escorted in by Knox and another guard. The armed guards were instructed to wait outside the gates, which they complied with.

Knox walked in with MacTavish, who described a battle between himself and the landowner to the south. Apparently the feud had taken a turn for the worse.

MACTAVISH'S VISIT TURNED out to be a favorable occurrence because when he was about to inform Alexander he was returning to the fishing village, the laird was heading out with the stout man in tow.

As Alexander exited the house along with his personal guard he stopped and told Knox, "McMurray's trial will have to wait until the morrow. I must see about this feud and possibly another to manage the lands next to MacTavish's, as those belong to Clan Ross."

"I plan to return to the fishing huts today. I am sure McMurray didnae kill Fitz," Knox informed his cousin.

Alexander had always been a fair man, but along with his title he carried the burden of ensuring justice was served. "See about it then."

KNOX RETURNED TO the great room crossing the space with

long strides past tables where people sat either waiting for an audience with Cynden, who now sat in Alexander's stead, or awaiting the next meal.

Clan Ross always fed those who were in the great room, whether there for an audience or not. Although the fare for those who didn't live there was not the same, the meal was good and filled empty stomachs.

When spotting Sencha's mother and her sister, he went to them. Both looked up with hope-filled expressions, only to return to worrying when he shook his head. "Nothing new as yet," he informed them. "The trial will be delayed for another day. My cousin had to go see about an urgent matter."

"Is that good news?" Sencha's aunt asked wrenching her hands.

Knox nodded. "I believe it could help. Perhaps witnesses can be found that will prove yer husband's innocence."

"Where is Sencha?"

Her mother shrugged, not seeming to be worried in the least. "I have nae been able to speak to her as yet. She got up early and has been off somewhere. Perhaps with Nala."

"I will find her and then head to the village to ask about any other witnesses." Knox didn't divulge his plans to go to the fishing huts, not wishing to give the already frayed women any false hope. It was probable, he'd not find out anything new that day.

Sencha was not with Nala or his aunt in the sitting room. Once he was satisfied she was not in the main house, he went out to the courtyard.

When nearing the storehouse, Fenella, a lass he'd been with in the woods, exited and upon seeing him walked directly toward him, with a purposeful sway to her hips and pout on her lips. "Ye have nae sought me out as of late. Should I be worried?" She traced a finger down his arm.

Fenella was a lustful wench, who'd always brought out the randy side of his personality. Unexplainably, this time he didn't find her as appealing.

"Have ye seen Sencha?" he asked without preamble. He could have replied to her question, but he was beginning to worry.

Fenella's bottom lip disappeared between her teeth, as she considered him. "She probably snuck away to meet a lover."

An uncontrollable flinch was impossible to hide, but he recovered quickly clearing his throat. "So ye saw her leaving the keep then?"

The lass shrugged. "I have nae seen her."

Without another word, Knox walked away. He didn't believe for one moment that Sencha had a lover or was in a courtship for that matter. However, it was possible that she'd met with someone to help her in the quest to help her uncle.

After searching the garden and behind the main house, he was sure Sencha was gone, and he had a good idea where the willful woman had gone to. Grinding his teeth together, he sent a lad to fetch his steed.

Hendry walked out from the stables pulling his horse behind, just as a stable hand brought out his horse. The young man looked at him and flushed. "I was to give ye a message, but I could nae find ye earlier. Then with the laird leaving…"

"What is it?" Knox interrupted, not really interested in what was probably a message from one of the many women who pursued him.

"A lass came earlier to get a horse," Thomas began and swallowed. "I forgot her name. She has red hair."

"Sencha?" Knox blurted out.

"Aye, that is it. She asked that I inform ye that she headed to the fishing huts."

Before the stable hand could continue, Knox grabbed the horse's reins. "How long ago?"

"Earlier this morning, around first meal."

Knox fought the urge to curse. It was obvious the boy had not tried to find him as he'd been in the practice fields for a while that morning. Not wishing to waste any more time, he mounted wordlessly.

"I will go with ye." Hendry mounted and they guided the steeds through the courtyard and past the gates.

Urging the mounts to a canter, they rode side by side, scanning the surroundings in case Sencha was about. He doubted she'd stopped until reaching the seashore.

"She is important to ye," Hendry stated glancing toward him. "Ye are aware that she is nae one to be played with."

"What makes ye say that?" Knox asked, genuinely interested in any observation Hendry had.

His friend chuckled. "The worry lines around yer mouth and the furrow of yer brow. The way ye constantly search for her when entering the great room. It is nae only me that has noted it."

"We need to hurry." Knox ignored Hendry's observations and prompted his mount to a gallop.

When they came to the fork in the road that would either take them to the village or to the seashore, they decided Hendry would go to the village and ask around both about

Sencha and for witnesses who may have seen McMurray that morning.

"While asking about for witnesses and see if ye can find them." Hendry lifted a hand in acknowledgement and urged his mount away leaving Knox to head in the other direction.

The air was cool across his face and Knox took in a deep breath. Had what Hendry said been the truth? Was he developing deep feelings for Sencha?

Of course he found her attractive, there was no denying the woman's beauty. She was small in stature, with soft curves and pert breasts. Then there were those expressive eyes of hers, thickly lashed green pools. Her lips were pink and plump, alluring and demanding attention. It was a miracle the woman hadn't yet been claimed.

Perhaps because she spent most of her days secluded at home with her mother, her only company until lately had been Nala. Now that Nala lived at the keep, Sencha visited regularly, which could only mean she would garner the attention of the many men there.

At the thought a protective urge surfaced taking him by surprise. Although at two and thirty, he was past the age to marry, he'd not given it much thought. He wasn't sure to be the type of man to settle any time soon.

His parents had not lived long enough for him to ken their story, having died when he was but a bairn of four or five. He'd come to live at his uncle's home, brought into the fold as one of five boys growing up together as brothers. Despite him not being treated any differently than Alexander, Munro, Gavin, and Cynden, he'd always known he was their cousin, the only child of their father's brother.

Both his uncle and aunt had doted on him, ensuring he never wanted for anything. Upon dying the late laird went so far as to deed him land and coin, ensuring his brother's son would never want for anything.

Still there had always been a hollow in his chest, a void left by his parents who'd died at sea. The fact that they would never return had yet to settle in his mind. How had they died? Why had fate been so unfair that they'd perished together? Knox would go weeks, months even without thinking about it. But then something would spark that feeling, bring back the hollow sensation that resided in his core. It was like a hunger that could never be fulfilled, not painful, but unable to be ignored.

Deep inside, he knew it was the reason why he couldn't settle. Couldn't marry. If the loss of his parents affected him for an entire lifetime, how much worse would it be to lose a wife?

Shaking himself from the pondering, he searched the seashore, his gaze scanning across the blue-gray expanse where the fishing boats floated atop. There were several far out to sea, barely visible, others remained closer.

From the shoreline, it was impossible to recognize who the men were and unless one recognized the boats and knew which belonged to whom, there was no way to tell who was out fishing that day.

THE FISHING HUTS came into view, most of them with doors closed and either mules or horses in attached pens. Carts that would take those who lived in town sat forlornly beside some of the huts. There were long tables crudely built to withstand the salty air and water, where the fishermen would clean the fish they'd caught. The planks of the table tied with sturdy ropes keeping them in place.

The wind whistled through the structures making an eerie sound, as he guided his horse to the long table and dismounted. The horse nudged him as if warning Knox to proceed with care. Reassuring the animal, he ran his palm down the long face. "All is well," he whispered to the horse.

There didn't seem to be anyone about until movement caught his attention. In the distance, an older man carried nets to a small boat. Knox jogged toward him, calling until the man looked up.

"Have ye seen a lass about?"

The fisherman shook his head. "Been feeling poorly and only just got up. I've nae seen anyone."

"Is there a lad with a missing front tooth about? I must speak to him," Knox tried again.

"That would be Willy. He comes and goes. Sometimes accompanies some of the fishermen out to earn coin."

Both looked out to the sea as if they would spot the boy. No one was close enough that they could see if a boy was aboard.

Knox handed the man a coin and returned to where his horse was tethered. Deciding it was best to have a look about in case the boy or Sencha were there, he made his way past the first line of huts.

Just as he turned a corner, a man he recognized as Kyle, walked out of hut. At seeing him the man's eyes widened. "What are ye doing here?" the man asked gruffly. "Dinnae think ye can steal anything. There is nothing worth taking."

Knox gave him a droll look. "I am searching for a boy called Willy."

The man's eyes shifted toward the hut he'd just walked out of and shrugged. "The boy comes and goes."

Knox kept his eyes on the other man's hands. "Ye were to be a witness at the trial, why are ye nae at the keep?"

Again the man's eyes shifted. "I have nothing more to say. Leave me be."

It wasn't worth his time. If the man would not come and testify, it would prove beneficial for Donald McMurray. By the jerky way the man moved he was hiding something, but in all probability, it had nothing to do with the murder, or with the lad.

Knox decided he would return to inspect the hut that this man was obviously trying to keep him from entering.

"We may return to ask ye more questions," Knox informed the man before turning away.

"And be hung. I will nae ever go. Fitz deserved to die."

Knox reached for his sword but as he started to turn back, a hard hit to the back of his head made him stumble forward.

The second, he barely felt.

CHAPTER FIVE

U PON WAKING SENCHA found it was hard to breathe, and when she tried to take in more than a small amount of air the result was dry hacking coughs which only made her lungs hurt worse. When she finally managed to pry her eyes open, they burned from the smoke-filled air, but she discovered she was lying on a cot. Tied up and facing a wall that was not well-built as there were slots between the planks of wood, she could make out sunlight and smell the sea air outside.

After another bout of coughing that felt nearly impossible to stop, she wiggled closer to the wall and pushed her mouth and nose between the slots. Sucking in the cleaner air felt like heaven as it eased the pressure in her lungs.

When she could finally manage a breath without choking, her thoughts were clearer sending the signals to her mind to assess the current situation.

Her feet were bound at the ankles and her hands tied securely behind her back. Once again she leaned forward and took in another lungful of air as she curled into a ball so that she could bring her hands to the front instead of behind her back.

Finally she managed to get her hands in front of her, then she began pulling at the rags around her ankles until she was able to loosen them. There was little she could do about the ties on her hands, but she only needed her feet to escape.

Once again the thick smoke made her throat seize and Sencha began coughing whilst looking around frantically attempting to find the front door. When she rushed toward the door her foot hit something on the floor sending her sprawling onto the dirt.

A man was on the floor. He was not bound but was unmoving. Either dead or passed out. The air was somewhat less smokey near the ground and she crawled back to the man, who lay between her and the door.

Upon recognizing the still man, she shook him. "Knox! Wake up!"

He didn't move sending her heart into a gallop. She pressed her ear to his mouth and was relieved to feel his breath. "Knox," she repeated, once again pushing her bound hands against his shoulder. "Please wake up."

Other than a dry cough, he didn't stir, and Sencha gave up trying to wake him. She'd have to drag him out, there was no other way.

Keeping low to the ground, she half-crawled to the door. Upon reaching the door, she pushed against it, but it didn't budge. The man who'd attacked her must have blocked it.

It was becoming harder to breathe, and the smoke was giving way to red flames. Sencha whirled when flames lapped through the far wall. She ran to a window, threw it open, and managed to climb out.

Tears streamed down her face, and her eyes burning so badly that she could barely stand to keep them open. Knox was still inside, and she had to save him.

Out of nowhere a boy rushed toward her, his wide eyes

taking in the structure.

She tried to speak but a hacking fit ensued. "H-help me... I have to get him out." Sencha managed between bouts of coughing.

"I can untie ye," the boy said pulling at the rags that had been used to bind her hands. It took some effort, but finally her wrists fell apart sending tingling sensations up her arms.

Together they managed to pull a heavy rock out of the way. Without hesitating she rushed into the hut, motioning for the lad to remain back. The boy was obviously not about to be told what to do, because he came up beside her and they grabbed the rough fabric across Knox's shoulders and began tugging him toward the door.

Although skinny, the boy was stronger than he seemed and with his help, they managed to drag Knox out the door just as the roof of the shack collapsed sending the flames and smoke higher into the darkening sky.

Sencha fell sideways onto the dirt coughing and wiping wildly at her stinging eyes.

"Ye are bleeding from yer face," the boy pointed out.

It was the least of her worries. Knox had yet to wake.

MEN CAME RUNNING, most of them screaming out orders to grab buckets to keep the fire from spreading to the other huts.

Both she and Knox were carried to the back of the wagon and a horse was hitched to it. She wasn't sure, but it may have been the boy who informed them that Knox was the laird's cousin.

Too exhausted to move, she sat hunched over with Knox's head on her lap watching all the activity.

A red stain on her skirt made her realize that Knox bled. The hair on the back of his head was matted with drying blood. She wanted to scream for the men to hurry, but her throat didn't allow for more than a hoarse whisper.

Since no one had asked who'd captured them, she hadn't volunteered the information. If any of them were in alliance with the man who'd attacked her, they could turn on her and at the moment neither she nor Knox would be able to defend themselves.

When a man walked toward them, Sencha curved protectively around Knox. The man looked at Knox. "He has nae wakened?"

Sencha shook her head. "We must get him to a healer." Her voice was barely above a hoarse whisper.

"Tom will take ye to the village now," the man said giving Knox a worried look.

A man on horseback appeared in the distance. By the size of the animal and rider, it was a warhorse and warrior. Sencha wanted to cry as he neared, and she recognized Hendry.

Bringing the horse animal to a stop, Hendry glanced down at Knox. "What happened?"

"Attacked by a man who burned down the shack hoping to kill us," Sencha managed to say past the soreness of her throat.

Hendry called over to the man who'd climbed onto the bench reins in hand. "To the keep. Fast."

BY THE TIME they crossed into the courtyard at the keep, Sencha was in so much pain she'd stopped trying to be brave and was crying. Not only was her face throbbing from the man's strikes, but each breath was painful. And she'd scratched both arms and legs whilst climbing out the window.

Her mother and aunt rushed out to the wagon along with several guards, and she was helped down. When trying to stand, she would have crumpled to the ground, if not for a guard catching her.

Hendry swept Sencha up into his arms and carried her into the house. Over his shoulder, she watched as Knox was taken from the back of the wagon and carried past them.

Moments later, Hendry placed her in a small bedchamber on the ground level. The trio of her mother, aunt, and Nala rushed into the room peppering her with questions.

When she began to cry, the questioning turned to soothing.

"Get some hot water and bandages," Nala instructed. "Ask Cook to boil tea with herbs to help with her pain."

There were scurrying of feet and other things said, but all Sencha could think about was Knox. What if he never woke? She had no idea who the man was that had attacked her and with all probability Knox as well.

By the way it was hard to see out of her left eye, she figured that side of her face was swollen from the man's strikes.

Her mother began washing her face, while her aunt did the same with her arms. Nala lingered at her feet, instructing servants to help undress her and wash her legs and feet.

Although her mother did her best to be gentle, each time her face was touched, she gasped at the pain.

"I could not bear to ever lose ye child," her mother whispered, her voice shaking with emotion. "God knew not to take ye from me. Losing ye would be unbearable."

Sencha tried to make light of the situation. "Ye would have

Athol and his stories of travel."

When her mother met her gaze, there was profound sadness. "I lost Athol when yer father died. He became another person, refusing to remain here and be part of the family. He feels guilty and until he resolves it, he will remain lost to us."

Whenever Athol visited, it was always brief. Usually no more than a pair of months, sometimes not even a fortnight. He spoke only of his travels, rarely asking about anyone who lived on Skye.

He'd been with their father on the day of the tragedy. Returning from the village a storm had occurred. A tree had fallen across the wagon, crushing them both. Athol's leg had been broken and yet he'd tried to free their father from under the tree.

They were found the next morning, Athol passed out and her father dead. It had been a tragedy, but for whatever reason, Athol had persisted that he should have been able to save their father.

Soon after, he'd joined Nala's brother Belhar at sea.

BY THE TIME they'd finished the tasks of cleaning her wounds, the effect of the herbs in the tea had helped to ease the pain.

It was late when the healer finally appeared. The man didn't speak much and seemed more bothered than concerned, but he was efficient. He had her right wrist bound.

"Ye will have to keep it bound for a fortnight," the healer stated, his gaze going over the injuries on her face. He must not have found them to need attention as he didn't do more.

"How is Knox?" Sencha asked, the sound of her voice still hoarse.

The healer looked to Nala as if for permission to speak. When she nodded, he replied, "He has yet to regain consciousness. With an injury to the head, one cannae predict what the outcome will be. Someone is to be with him constantly so as to alert me when he awakens."

THE HERBS MUST have taken effect, because when Sencha next opened her eyes it was dark outside. In the bedchamber the only light came from the feeble fire in the hearth. Obviously everyone had gone to bed, and she was glad for it as her mother and aunt had planned to remain in constant vigil over her for hours.

No one had come to ask about the attacker. Nala must have instructed that she was not to be bothered. Perhaps the boy or one of the other fishermen had known who the shack belonged to and had informed the laird.

Her mind turned to Knox. He'd been so still, his body without life or movement. Had the smoke caused more damage to his already badly injured head?

If only she'd not gone alone to the fishing village. Despite the dangerous man attacking her and being the one who'd caused injury, perhaps it would not have happened if she'd not gone there.

Had Knox gone to the shoreline to search for her? Would he have gone anyway as part of his quest to find witnesses?

The only person who knew for sure was him and perhaps Hendry. She'd have to speak to him the next morning.

A thought occurred and she lifted a bandaged hand to her mouth. Her uncle's trial. Had it happened yet? She'd not thought to ask her aunt.

Surely if the trial had occurred and the result had been bad, her aunt would have been overly distraught and that had not been the case.

Morning could not get around fast enough, there were so many questions she needed answers to.

UNABLE TO SETTLE, she sat up and swung her feet over the side of the bed. Her chest ached from the activity, but it wasn't as painful as before.

Gingerly she lowered her feet to the floor, the stones were cold, but not too bothersome. Sencha reached for a robe left by Nala if she were to guess.

Once she donned the robe, she made her way slowly to the door and opened it.

The corridor was empty, the only light came from a lantern on a small shelf. It was enough for her to see there were two other doors and nothing more.

She went from the room, keeping a hand on the wall for balance as she made her way to the first door. Slowly as to not awaken whoever was inside, she cracked the door open and peeked in.

A thick muscled man sat in a chair, his gaze on the fire. On the bed was Knox, who looked to be asleep. The guard must have sensed her because he turned and looked to the doorway.

"I want...need to see how he fares," Sencha whispered.

The man motioned her forward. "He has yet to wake." He stood and stretched. "I am Torrance. If ye will remain a few moments, I must go fetch something and return shortly."

Sencha guessed the man needed to relieve himself. "Aye, of course. Take yer time."

The man hurried from the room, and she hobbled to the side of the bed lowering to sit on it.

Several strands of thick burnished hair fell over Knox's brow, and she brushed them aside. Despite his handsome features, even in repose he was an intimidating warrior.

His eyelids flickered and Sencha bent to get a closer look. "Knox. Can ye hear me?" she whispered.

The movement happened again, and he coughed. "All is well. Ye are back in the keep," Sencha said. "Ye were attacked, and he burned the shack both of us were trapped in."

This time he let out a soft groan.

Remembering how horribly thirsty she'd been upon leaving the burning shack, Sencha reached for the pitcher on the bedside table and poured the liquid into a cup. Gently she lifted Knox's head and dribbled some past his parted lips.

He swallowed giving her incentive to continue to pour small amounts into his mouth. Finally, he turned his head away signaling he'd had his fill.

"Fetch Alex." His voice was hoarse, barely above a whisper.

"It is late at night. We can get him in the morning," Sencha told him while brushing his hair back away from his face. Although unnecessary, she needed to keep touching him, to ensure he was indeed alive and now awake.

The guard finally returned, and Sencha looked over her shoulder at him. "He is awake. Does the healer wish to be called?"

As if it needed verification, the guard neared the bed. "Knox?"

Knox coughed and nodded.

The man walked out and left them alone again. Sencha

pressed a gentle kiss to Knox's brow. "I am so glad ye woke. Everyone has been so worried."

Finally his eyes opened and met hers. When they widened, Sencha knew he could make out her injuries despite the dimness of the room.

"What happened?"

She flinched thinking of the sight she must be. "The man who attacked ye, had already bound me and put me in the shack which he later set on fire."

"He is called Kyle."

A disheveled healer burst into the room, behind him a sleepy young man who Sencha supposed was his assistant.

He stopped abruptly at seeing Sencha. "Ye should nae be out of bed." Looking to his assistant, he motioned with his hand toward the door. "Help her back to her chamber."

Left with no choice, Sencha stood and looked down at Knox, but his eyes were closed again.

CHAPTER SIX

I F EVER HE'D had a headache that bad, Knox could not remember it. With even the slightest movement, his head pounded from the temples to the back of his skull where the healer informed him there'd been an open gash that had to be sewn shut.

After slowly getting up from the bed and dressing in clothes that had been left out for him, he winced when having to bend over and put on his boots.

First stop would be the kitchen where he'd ask Cook for something for the pain, after he had to speak to Alexander who'd yet to come to see him.

Whatever the issue was at the bordering lands must have kept him occupied because according to Hendry, the laird had not returned until late the night before.

As he walked out into the corridor, Hendry appeared with a cup in his hand. "I was coming to bring ye this. It is for the pain."

Relief flooded him as he reached for it. "Hopefully it will nae make me sleepy." He drank the entire contents in three swallows and closed his eyes willing the headache to go away.

"Where are ye headed?" Hendry said taking the empty cup.

"I must speak to Alexander. The man who attacked Sencha and me is called Kyle. A fisherman. I believe he is related to the dead man, Fitz."

Hendry nodded. "I ken of him. Do ye think he killed Fitz and that is why he attacked ye?"

"He said something to make me believe that he did. I must have caught him as he planned to flee or because he'd captured Sencha and didnae wish for me to find out."

"Nonetheless, he tried to kill ye both and for that he must be punished." Hendry turned on his heel and hurried away. The warrior would gather a group of men and head out to hunt for Kyle. There was no need to wait for the laird to order it.

Continuing past a door, he wondered if it was where Sencha was. He hoped to see her and speak to her, assure himself that she was better. Her face had been badly bruised, one eye almost swollen shut. Once they caught Kyle, he would ensure the bastard paid for what he did to the woman.

Just as he turned to knock on the door, a servant woman he'd once seduced came from the end of the corridor. Upon seeing him, she rushed to meet him. "Should ye be out of bed?"

Knox accepted her help, mainly because he wasn't sure he'd be able to remain upright much longer as whatever Cook had concocted was making him feel dizzy.

"Poor dear, let me help ye to bed," the woman insisted and turning with him to head back toward the room he'd just walked out of.

Sencha stood at the door, her eyes glued to where the servant was tucked under his arm.

"How do ye fare?" Knox asked leaning heavily on the woman beside him. "Yer swelling has lessened some."

"I am fine," Sencha replied, her voice still a hoarse whisper. With that she walked into the corridor and past them.

"Come ye are quite unsteady," the servant prompted, urging him to continue toward the room.

Knox extricated himself from her and put a hand on the wall to steady himself. "Can ye find Alexander and tell him I must speak to him at once?"

"Aye," she replied, her eyes taking him in as if expecting that he might fall at any moment.

"Go now."

The woman hurried away, and Knox leaned against the wall weighing his options of whether he should try to make it to the great room or wait for Alexander in the bedchamber.

Sencha entered the great room scanning the area until she found her mother and aunt. Both sat at a table with Nala and the laird's mother. There was tension in the room as the people waited for whatever the witnesses would say in favor or against her uncle.

Several people turned to look at her, their eyes glued to what she was sure was not a pretty sight. Although she'd not looked in a mirror, she'd felt her face and noted swelling and a lump on her jaw. Ignoring the stares, she went to the table where her mother sat and lowered to the bench.

Immediately someone placed a cup of ale, and a bowl filled with a thick soup, for her to break her fast. Despite the dread about what was going to happen, her stomach grumbled with expectation.

"Eat my darling." Her mother reached for her hand. "At the moment, the laird is listening to another issue."

She was surprised when a moment later, the servant who'd been helping Knox entered and hurried to the front of the room. Without waiting to be summoned forward, she neared the laird and whispered into his ear.

Alexander nodded and replied to the woman who then walked back heading in the direction she'd come. No doubt she'd delivered a message from Knox.

Sencha wondered if the servant and Knox had ever been romantically involved. The thought made her stomach clench. Unsure when it had happened, but her feelings for Knox had changed radically. No longer did she see him as a friend. When he'd become her family's champion helping to find the truth and defending her uncle, she'd begun to see him in a different light.

Her attraction to him had always been there, as there was no denying that she'd always found him handsome. But it was his reputation as a rogue that had put her off.

Sencha was surprised that her bowl was empty, she'd eaten every bit whilst considering what would happen next with her uncle. She would step up and tell everyone about being attacked when she'd gone to the fishing village to find the lad who was a possible witness.

It was not proof of his guilt, but it certainly shed light on the possibility that the man who attacked her and Knox was the same man who killed the fisherman.

The boy who'd helped her the day before had to be the one she sought. She wished she'd asked the boy to come to the keep, but her mind had been in a fog and all she'd been thinking about was saving Knox and getting him to a healer.

She'd not even asked the boy's name. Nor did she ken the

identity of the man who'd attempted to burn her and Knox alive.

Murmurs got her attention, and she turned to see her uncle's heartbreaking appearance. He looked small and feeble walking forward between two warriors with swords strapped to their backs and daggers tucked into their belts.

Surely all those weapons were not necessary for the task at hand. It could be, she considered, that they always wore the weaponry. Still, it made her feel so sad for her poor, sweet uncle.

As he walked by, her aunt jumped to her feet and rushed to him, but one of the warriors stuck out an arm to stop her. Despite the gesture, the warrior gave her aunt an apologetic look. "Please sit."

Her uncle didn't speak, his eyes pinned to his wife, his expression that of resignation. Sencha lifted her hand palm toward him and smiled hoping to give him encouragement. He didn't seem to notice.

As the trio of men made their way to the front of the room, the murmuring got louder. People speculating. Stating opinions about the outcome. Some even going so far as to jeer at her uncle. Sencha bunched her hands in an effort to keep calm and not confront anyone.

Her mother must have sensed her anger because she covered Sencha's hand with her own. "All will be well. It has to be."

If only it was that easy.

When the laird stood, everyone went silent. Alexander was a tall man, and standing on the high board, he towered over the warriors and her uncle. He peered down at her uncle.

"Donald McMurray, ye stand here accused of murder. The death of a man called Fitz."

No one said anything, as there was no question asked.

Then the laird studied those gathered. "This is a matter of great importance. If ye wish to remain in this room, keep silent. I will nae hesitate in having ye removed from here."

There was still a smattering of murmurs. It seemed the people were having a hard time keeping silent, Alexander gave the room a hard look and silence quickly descended.

Once the room was silent, the laird motioned to her uncle. "What have ye to say?"

"I didnae kill Fitz, my laird. I went that morning to the fishing village only to return the knife I had borrowed from a fisherman called Guiles. I swear to ye my laird, I never saw Fitz." Her uncle's voice wavered slightly, but he spoke out loudly.

"How do ye ken the dead man?" Alexander asked, still standing.

"I often go to the fishing village to get fish. My wife and I like to eat fish."

At this point the laird sat and looked to his scribe. "Who are the witnesses?"

Several people raised their hands, Sencha included, who waved hers wildly.

The first person chosen to speak was a man Sencha didn't recognize. By his weathered face and shabby clothing, she guessed him to be a fisherman.

"My laird, I am called Hugh. I saw Fitz arguing with a man two days before dying. The man was taller than him. They shoved each other."

Murmurs grew but stopped suddenly at the laird's sharp look around the room. "Who was the man he fought with?"

The man shifted nervously. "I was too far out on the water to see clearly. My eyes are nae what they use to be."

What the man had said was helpful, and Sencha was glad it was not someone who would make her uncle seem guilty.

The laird finally looked in her direction. "Come forth, Sencha."

When she stood there were gasps and exclamations about her appearance. Sencha did her best to keep her composure. In a way she was glad not to have looked in a mirror, at the same time not knowing made her want to crawl under one of the tables.

"How are ye faring?" Alexander's expression was etched with concern.

"B-better. I wish to speak about what happened yesterday. I went to the fishing village to seek out the boy who may have seen something. He is called Willy. I was attacked by a man. He wanted to stop me from finding the boy."

The whispers in the room swirled around her like a steady breeze. She shivered not wanting to hear what was said. "My laird. I can describe the man. I dinnae ken his name, but he is taller than my uncle and…"

"Ye ken nothing then?" someone jeered.

"A woman alone at the fishing village attacked has naught to do with this," someone else said.

Alexander's gaze didn't waver from her. "Did the man say anything about Fitz that makes ye think he was who killed him?"

She wanted to cry. "Nae. He also attacked yer cousin,

Knox. He has to be who murdered Fitz. Why else would he try to kill us?"

By the laird's lack of expression, Sencha knew it barely helped. At the same time, what happened to her and Knox at the hands of the man had to cast doubt about her uncle being who killed the man Fitz.

Alexander dismissed her, and she turned to look at her uncle, who managed a soft smile and mouthed the words, *thank ye*. She shuffled back to the table where both her mother and aunt took her hands.

"There is little evidence for or against this man, Donald McMurray. Where is the man Kyle, who supposedly witnessed the accused of coming from the direction of the dead man's hut?"

"He will nae appear," Knox stated in a hoarse voice as he was helped by a guard toward the front of the room. "He is who attacked Sencha and me and tried to burn us alive."

At the statement there were audible gasps and people began talking over each other.

"Silence," Alexander called out in a strong, deep voice. "Enough." He turned to his cousin. "Someone help him to sit."

A chair was dragged next to Knox, but he remained standing. "Just before striking me, Kyle stated that he would nae come forward and be hung and that Fitz deserved to die."

Once again the people began speaking, but this time kept their voices low, obviously not wishing to miss whatever was said next.

"He must be found," Alexander said.

"Hendry and Liam have already gone with several men to search for him. He cannae have gone far. However, he does have a boat." Knox went into a fit of coughs and had to lower to the chair.

"Take all the bìrlinns out," Alexander commanded to several warriors who rushed out of the room. He then spoke to her uncle directly. "I dinnae believe ye killed Fitz. I find ye innocent of the crime ye are accused of."

Her uncle seemed to sag with relief, tears streaming down his face. "Thank ye, Laird. I assure ye, I am innocent."

Along with her aunt and mother, Sencha rushed to the front of the room to hug her uncle, who hugged his wife tightly as they both cried.

HER MOTHER, AUNT, and uncle walked from the room in the direction of the door. No doubt her uncle and aunt wished nothing more than to return home and she didn't blame them one bit. Sencha herself wished to go home and recover from her injuries away from prying eyes.

Turning around, she noticed that Knox had sagged into the chair and looked on as people went to the laird. In all probability, they were Fitz's friends and family asking for justice.

She neared and lowered to her knees in front of Knox. "Thank ye. Ye saved my uncle's life and almost lost yers in the process."

When he met her eyes, he half-smiled. "And ye saved my life. I would say we are even." Taking her shoulder he attempted to help her to stand and then winced and closed his eyes.

Sencha leaned closer cupping his face with both hands. "Yer head continues to hurt. Ye should go lie down. I will help ye."

When he opened his eyes and gazed into hers, it was as if the room emptied and only he and she existed. She couldn't help looking down at his lips, wondering what it would be like for them to press against hers. It was as if time stood still, neither able to formulate words nor move away.

"I will help ye back to yer room," a deep voice said immediately breaking the spell.

Knox blinked and nodded, once again wincing. "I can walk," he said looking up at the guard who stood by.

"Again, thank ye," Sencha said and pressed a kiss to his cheek. "My family is forever in yer debt."

CHAPTER SEVEN

HENDRY RODE AWAY from the village to search the nearby woods. No one had seen Kyle, and the search was beginning to frustrate him. It was impossible that the man could have gone so far as to not be caught. In his haste to leave the fishing village, he'd left all of his belongings, taking another man's horse and perhaps a blanket.

The man's small boat remained at the shoreline, and no one reported theirs or even Fitz's boat missing.

As annoyed as he was, Hendry was determined to find the man even if it meant staying out for days. He was used to surviving off the land and foraging for food. Not that he would have to go very far before being able to find a meal. The clan's people would not hesitate to feed one of the laird's guardsmen.

A small cottage came into view and noticing nothing askew he approached it. Beside the cottage was a neat garden where a woman tilled the soil. So intent on her task, she didn't see him until he was almost upon her.

Her dog must have made a sound because she straightened and at seeing him her eyes narrowed; then she continued to work, not paying him any heed. Unlike her, the large black dog—who was her steady companion—stood and growled. The deep sound menacing.

Hendry dismounted and remained by his horse whilst

eyeing the dog.

"What do ye want?" Ailith Shaw brushed a strand of dark brown hair away from her face with the back of her hand.

When the dog growled again, she shushed him in a low whisper, "Hush, Teller." The dog kept his steady gaze on Hendry.

"Ye should be with care. There is a man in hiding who killed a man at the fishing village."

She put her hoe down and walked out of the fenced in area, her dog steadily beside her. "What happened?"

As the woman neared, Hendry couldn't help noticing the sway of her ample hips and her graceful strides. She had large hazel eyes that contrasted with her tan skin and deep brown hair. Her mouth was just a bit big for her face, but somehow it complemented her features, making her more alluring.

They'd never been on friendly terms, mainly because her now-deceased husband and Hendry had not gotten along.

Both were guards in service to the laird, and her husband had been killed in battle against the Mackinnons, a rival clan that Clan Ross had overcome. Unfortunately there were a few deaths on both sides, which included Ailith's husband Brant. Since Hendry and Brant had not gotten along, somehow, she placed the blame on him.

He'd not been in the same area, but that mattered little to the distraught widow. He understood. It was a way to help with the pain; to place blame on someone.

"A fisherman called Fritz was stabbed to death. The man suspected of killing him, Kyle, has gone into hiding. We think he remains on the isle."

Ailith looked around, her face etched with worry. "Do ye

think he is near here?"

The urge to both protect her and soothe her mind overtook Hendry. Admittedly, one of the reasons he'd never gotten along with Brant was because of Ailith. He'd planned to court her and had told the man. Then when Hendry had been sent away to the Isle of Uist, Brant had gone after Ailith. Hendry always suspected it was only to best him and not because the other warrior actually was in love with Ailith that he'd courted her.

When Ailith huffed impatiently getting his attention, Hendry met her gaze. "I dinnae ken where he is. I am tracking him, and it looks as if he may have headed in this direction."

With a shrug as if unconcerned, she reached for her dog's head and patted it. "Teller will keep me safe."

His look of doubt must have been evident because Ailith lifted a brow and pulled a dagger from the folds of her skirt. "I also have this and my wits."

"Yer wits are sharper than that blade," Hendry said with a grin. "The words ye have thrown at me in the past have cut quite deeply."

When she looked up to the sky and back to him, she seemed to relax some. "It is in the past. Although I will admit that I dinnae care for ye Hendry, in the least."

"I am more than aware, Ailith," he replied. "It will nae deter me from protecting ye and ensuring ye are nae harmed."

For a moment he thought she was going to rebut with an unkind comment, but instead she huffed out a breath. "Thank ye for informing me." She turned back toward the garden without a backward glance.

Hendry considered lingering and asking for water, just to

remain there a few moments longer. However, he'd been summarily dismissed and when she began working again without looking back up, he decided it was best to leave well enough alone. He would circle the area to ensure Kyle was nowhere near there and then continue his search for the fleeing man.

"I will search the area," he called out to the woman who continued to ignore him.

THEY HAD BEEN given a choice: stay within the safety of the keep or return home under the watchful eye of two guards. Given that Sencha had been attacked by Kyle, the council feared he might seek her out again. Though she doubted it—convinced the man had no clue who she truly was. However, her mother's fear had been another matter entirely. To ease her mother's anxiety, Sencha had reluctantly agreed to remain at the keep until Kyle was found and captured.

Her mother, pale and visibly shaken, had gone upstairs to rest in the room they shared, leaving Sencha to her own thoughts. She meandered to the back of the main house in search of fresh air and peace. A kind servant with a knowing smile, neared. "Come I will show ye a place away from prying eyes."

The young woman led Sencha through a rear door of the keep's main hall. Beyond it lay a small, secluded garden tucked against the stone walls, just out of sight from the bustling courtyard. A perfect place where she could escape the pitying glances and hushed whispers of those who noticed her bruised face and the swelling along her jaw.

The garden was a haven, quiet and sunlit. Birds flitted through the branches of nearby trees, their cheerful songs weaving through the soft rustle of leaves. Sencha tipped her face to the rare warmth of the autumn sun, letting its golden rays chase away the lingering chill in her bones. It was a rare gift for so late in the season, and she intended to savor it.

Thankfully, the worst of the pain had faded. She no longer needed to press cold cloths to her eye, and her jaw only ached when she attempted to chew. Soups would become her staple for the next few days. She'd go to the kitchen and prepare them herself, if only to feel some measure of control in the midst of so much chaos.

But peace was fleeting. As the quiet wrapped around her, her mind replayed the events of her captivity. The dark hut. The overwhelming silence broken only by the sound of her own shallow breathing. Kyle had left her there, alone and in agony, for what felt like an eternity. When he finally returned, it was as if madness clung to him like a shadow. He had paced the confines of the small space, his movements erratic, his muttering unintelligible. And then, to her horror, he had struck himself. Fists pounding against his head as if to exorcise some unseen demon.

Sencha closed her eyes, shuddering at the memory. She needed time to think, to piece together the fragments of what had happened. Kyle had offered no hints as to where he had been or what he had planned. All she had were fleeting images, moments of his erratic behavior, and the quiet dread that settled in her chest whenever she thought of him.

The sunlight couldn't banish all shadows, but here in the

garden, surrounded by the rustle of leaves and the gentle hum of life, she could breathe—just for a little while.

Once again the scene inside the fishing hut returned. While the man repeated words like, *he's dead* and *unfair*, he'd begun packing a small sack with a rolled blanket and a few meager possessions, including a knife.

When he'd looked in her direction, Sencha closed her eyes hoping he thought her still unconscious. Fear like she'd never known had made her shiver and tears stream down her face. Thankfully the man must have heard or seen Knox because he'd not hurt her further. Instead, he'd gagged her and gone out.

A familiar figure appeared just across from where she was. Sencha lowered to a bench and peered over the wall to see what he did. It was Knox and he stood surrounded by several men, probably his archers.

Surprising that he was out and about. Surely the healer had not allowed it.

The sound of their deep voices intermingled with the birdsong and the rustling of wind through the leaves making it hard to hear exactly what they spoke of.

Knox seemed to be giving directions because he pointed toward the front of the house and the rear. From what she knew, his team was made mostly of archers. At the moment all but two of the gathered men had bows strapped across their backs.

The men separated into three groups each heading in the direction Knox had ordered. He turned as if hearing his name being called and Sencha almost stood to wave him over. She needed to ken the progress of the search for the man who'd attacked them.

However, she stilled at seeing the woman from the village called Anni hurrying toward him. The flirty village woman had been lingering about the keep for a pair of days. Surely she had chores to tend to. And why weren't her parents sending for her?

Sencha pressed her teeth together watching as the woman neared Knox and began talking. The high octave of Anni's voice meant Sencha could hear her clearly.

"The healer will be most cross. Ye need to be abed."

When Knox replied, Sencha could not hear him as clearly. She let out an annoyed huff, not just for her inability to hear, but because she wasn't sure what urged her to be spying on them in the first place.

"We should go inside so ye can rest," Anni said and lifted to her toes leaning forward as if to kiss Knox. He took her by the shoulders stopping her. Again he said something Sencha couldn't hear.

The village girl laughed. A tinny sound that was not at all humorous. It was apparent she'd not appreciated the rebuff. The woman lingered for a moment before reluctantly turning and walking away.

Knox turned toward the house and Sencha shifted away hoping he'd not noticed her then chided herself. He was an archer with the keen vision of a bird of prey. If she was visible in any way, he would see her.

And he must have because moments later, he entered the garden.

Sencha lowered her head allowing her hair to fall forward. She'd finally looked in a mirror and had winced at seeing herself. Her eye was no longer swollen shut, but a blueish bruise surrounded it. Another large bruise covered the bottom half of the left side of her face. In addition, there was a cut on her chin that had happened either when the man had struck her or when she'd fought to escape.

Knox lowered to the bench and sat next to her. They sat in silence for a while, the only sounds were those of the birds and the voices that the wind carried from the courtyard.

"I wish I could go out with the men to search for the man who hurt ye." Knox's voice remained hoarse, but he spoke louder than he had that morning.

"He hurt ye as well," she said before peeking sideways at him through her hair. "The sun will be setting soon. Since warriors have nae returned with him, he must have evaded being caught."

"Aye."

Letting out a long breath, Sencha fought not to ask him about Anni but failed miserably. "Anni is pretty." Sencha wanted to flinch at the comment.

"She is," Knox replied.

"Are ye planning to court her?" Why couldn't she keep from asking? Apparently the hit on her head had impeded her ability to control her tongue and keep her from making a fool out of herself.

When he nudged her with his shoulder, Sencha turned to him. "Lift yer face up. I have never known ye to be one who cowers or hides."

"I am nae hiding," Sencha snapped.

"Ye are. I saw yer face when it was worse. Ye are recovering quickly."

He'd not answered her question and Sencha bit her tongue to keep from stating it out loud. Instead she glanced at him. "Does yer head still hurt?"

His broad shoulders lifted and lowered. "A bit, aye. The only reason I dinnae go out there is because I dinnae wish to hinder the search by not keeping up."

"It is commendable that ye recognize it and nae allow pride to take over," Sencha said.

Once again they fell into a companionable silence and Sencha was content to remain there, next to the strong archer. She wondered if he could tell her feelings for him had changed. It was doubtful, she'd done her best to keep them hidden.

"Ye are a brave and loyal woman." Knox's words shook her from her contemplation.

"I am nae brave. It was stupid of me to have gone to the fishing village without asking for an escort."

Once again he nudged her shoulder with his. The gesture was becoming his way of acknowledging her, it seemed. "I ken bravery when I see it. Not only did ye confront the man, but ye risked yer life to save mine."

A feeling of pride filled her at his words, and she lifted a shoulder and lowered it. "I could nae very well leave ye there to burn to a crisp, could I?"

"Ye could have. I wasn't an easy burden for ye I am sure."

"Very true, it felt as if I was dragging a bag of boulders. The poor lad did his best to help, but I had to do most of the work."

Knox frowned. "Once I recover, ye and I will go find the lad so I can reward him."

This time when they were silent again, Sencha felt awkward and stood. "I best go see about my mother."

Standing, Knox stretched both arms over his head and blew out a long breath. "I best go find the healer."

"Do as he says," Sencha told him.

When she turned, Knox took her arm stopping her, and when Sencha looked up to ask why, he kissed her. The kiss was soft and at the same time almost as if he were claiming her. Not daring to move, she remained still as he turned his head sideways and moved his lips over hers. Sencha wanted to grab his shoulders and pull him closer. But somehow she was strong enough to resist.

Lifted up just far enough to look into her eyes, he spoke. "There is only one lass I am considering courting for marriage, and it is nae Anni."

Sencha could feel her eyes widen at the slight tightness on her left side. Recalling her injuries and stepped back and ensured a bland expression. "Hmm, well I have heard said that most women would fall at yer feet."

"Would ye?" he teased.

"Absolutely not." With that, she turned on her heel and hurried away. She wasn't sure, but she thought to have heard him chuckle.

CHAPTER EIGHT

Two days later

KNOX WOKE AND sat up. For the first time, his head was clear and there was no headache. Tentatively, he slid to the edge of the bed and stood. His head remained clear and without pain. With a smile, he dressed then went to the window and pushed open the shutters to look out.

It was early yet and there was little movement in the courtyard. There had been no progress in finding Kyle. There was talk that he must have evaded capture by going to the mainland of Scotland. Somehow making it past the reinforcements sent by Alexander and those provided by his other cousin, Munro, who lived closer to the border.

Soon the day would arrive that Sencha and her mother would return to their home. It was inevitable, and he hated that they would be living in a house that offered little protection, other than a pair of farmhands.

As of yet, he had not identified what he felt for Sencha. Although the need to protect her had surged in him, he wasn't sure what it meant. He had no intention of settling down, yet, if ever. To allow any more impulses like the one in the garden would mean she'd expect something from him. Courtship and the like. Something he had never done. Recalling the words he'd spoken to her, he frowned. Whatever had made him say it?

Over the years he'd kissed and seduced many women, even believing himself to be in love with several, but the feelings had always disappeared. With Sencha, he'd admired her for years without his interest in her ever waning. Perhaps it was because he'd not had her. And yet, the simple soft almost friendly kiss between them had shaken him. He'd wanted more. Had wanted to pull her closer and kiss her until they were breathless.

What was different? Was it that it wasn't just sexual with her? No. This time it was different. He wanted to be close to her. To see her every day. Which he had made sure happened ever since the kiss.

He'd walked by and greeted her every morning, every afternoon, and every night. During meals, he'd managed to sit where he could watch her interact with the other women at the table. He'd not missed any opportunity to speak to her, even when she was accompanied.

Her mother had begun to cast suspicious glances in his direction, but he'd pretended not to notice, averting his gaze from Sencha, pretending interest in other people in the room.

Whatever was happening, he had to put an immediate stop to it. The last thing he wished for was to give Sencha the wrong impression.

Upon entering the great room, he groaned inwardly when he immediately searched the room for Sencha. She was not there, and neither was her mother.

Had they left?

Just then the scent of something sweet and floral wafted over to him and he turned to see Sencha make her way from the staircase. She smiled broadly and he turned so swiftly to look who she directed the smile at that his neck cracked.

Hendry walked to her and greeted her with a wide grin. "Sencha, ye look much better."

"I feel better," she replied good-naturedly. Then she noticed Knox and her cheeks pinkened and she returned her attention to Hendry.

Good for them, Knox wanted to actually mean it, but the tightness in his gut at seeing her with his friend made him want to punch Hendry.

"Thank ye, I may take ye up on the offer. I do feel the need for fresh air." Sencha said making her way in Knox's direction.

Just then Hendry noticed him and gave a friendly wave before walking toward the courtyard.

Her face was not as swollen, yet the remnants of the attack remained. The swelling was all but gone, only a bit of purpling remained beneath her left eye and in her jaw area.

"Do ye feel better?" Sencha asked lifting her gaze up to meet his.

"I am well," Knox replied. "What was that about?" He asked motioning toward the door where Hendry had just walked out through.

For a moment she looked confused and then seemed to realize what he asked about. "I asked Hendry the other day to let me ken if he was able to escort me for a walk outside the gates. Nala said he often accompanies her and Ainslie out."

"I dinnae think it safe for ye to be out alone with only one guard as yet."

At her crestfallen expression he wanted to take the words back. "I am sure we will find Kyle soon. Then ye will be free to do as ye wish… with Hendry or… with me." He gave her what he knew to be a grin that often got him anything he wanted from women.

Seeming unfazed, Sencha straightened and looked him in the eyes. "I dinnae have to listen to ye. If I wish to go for a walk, then I will." There was challenge in her green eyes. "Would ye allow me to pass? I am very hungry."

Unsure what to say in response, he stepped sideways, and she brushed past.

KNOX, ALONG WITH Cynden, Hendry, and another leader called Liam sat in Alexander's study. The room with its simple furnishings was at odds with the ornate chair the laird now sat in. It had been a gift to the late laird from a wealthy merchant in appreciation for Clan Ross's protection when the man's ships arrived on the northern shore.

"Other than the search for Kyle, we must ensure to keep men patrolling the border next to the Grant's lands," Alexander stated. "Although we are on friendly terms, I dinnae wish to give them the impression we are complacent."

Hendry spoke next. "There is no sign of Kyle anywhere. If he is in hiding, there must be someone helping him."

"I thought of that," Knox interjected. "It may be that we have to search house by house."

Alexander frowned. "I dinnae like to do it. People will resent it. However, if someone is harboring that man, whether willingly or not, it is best we find out."

Everyone waited as the laird pondered what had to be done.

"We can begin by asking for permission to enter. Just one

guard, non-threatening," Knox added.

"Do it," Alexander replied. "Start at the village, those who live there and nearby. I have a feeling he didnae go far."

As the men stood to go and instruct their teams, Alexander stopped him. "Knox, please stay back."

Knox sat back down and waited for the others to leave.

"Do ye feel well enough to ride?" Alexander's concern was both annoying and endearing.

"I do," Knox replied. "I am anxious to find this man and see him punished."

His cousin nodded in understanding. "I think Sencha and her mother should remain here. Nala is worried about them returning home and I do not like to see my wife upset."

Unable to keep from it, Knox grinned. "Ye are deeply under her spell, cousin."

"And I dinnae deny it," Alexander replied, grinning back. "I will ride with ye. When do ye plan to ride out?"

"First I will eat something," Knox acknowledged. "I missed first meal."

At Alexander's questioning look, Knox shrugged. "I was on my way in when ye called us in here." It was partly true, he'd not gone into the great room behind Sencha, opting instead to speak to Hendry. He'd informed Hendry that he was not to take Sencha out for a walk.

Not only was the lass still recovering, but it was dangerous if the man who'd attacked her was nearby. What he'd said was true, although if he were to be honest, he didn't like the idea of Sencha alone with Hendry.

The warrior had shrugged as if it were nothing important. It made Knox wonder if Hendry was not as interested romantically in Sencha as Knox had thought. He'd almost asked, but stopped, not wanting to give Hendry fodder that could be used against him in jest.

WHEN ASSIGNMENTS WERE handed out, Knox, Alexander, and two warriors had been given the area just east of the village. It contained several farms, along with a few cottages.

It was a pair of hours before they arrived at the first cottage. There didn't seem to be anyone about, so they approached the cottage and Knox dismounted.

At approaching the door, a man opened it and looked at him and then to the others. "What is it?"

"There is a man who is accused of murder in hiding. I wish to ensure ye and yer family are unharmed," Knox stated, looking past the man's shoulders to the interior.

Inside a woman sat by the hearth, a young child on her lap. When she met his eyes, it was obvious she was anxious. He wondered if her husband beat her.

THE MAN NODDED, again looking past him to the other three mounted men for a scant second. "We are well. No one has come here or approached us. He glanced over his shoulder to his family. "I will keep them inside and keep watch."

"Perhaps he went out to sea," his wife added, her voice shaky.

The man glanced over his shoulder. "Will we be notified when he is captured?"

Knox nodded. "Aye, men will be sent out to ensure everyone is aware."

They approached several other homes with similar results. Knox's neck and shoulders ached from frustration.

"He could nae have just disappeared," he gritted out. "The man is not that wily to evade all of our guardsmen."

Alexander scanned the surroundings, his expression grim. "Why would he kill Fitz? It seems most people had a good opinion of the dead man."

"Kyle is filled with hate. I believe him to be mad," Knox replied.

Upon approaching a house surrounded by fields, they once again neared, and Knox dismounted. A woman opened the door, her eyes moving from him to Alexander and the other warriors. "What happens?"

Knox related the same information he'd given the other people. She let out a long breath. "I have nae seen anyone about."

Effectively dismissing him, she closed the door before he could say anything more.

He mounted and glanced back at the house. "I supposed we should return, nothing else in the area."

Alexander motioned to the two warriors. "Ride to my brother's lands and ensure a search continues. Sleep there and return in the morning."

The pair of men rode off.

Urging their mounts forward, Knox looked to Alexander. "The woman may be right. If Kyle left right after setting the hut on fire, he could have gone past the inlet and out to sea. The search for him didn't commence until after I came to, which was late the next day."

"I have thought the same," Alexander responded. "Let us wait for the others to return. I will give the search another day and then call it off. Patrols can keep an eye out for him after tomorrow."

"What of Sencha and her mother?" Knox asked, immediately annoyed with himself.

Alexander's brows rose when he looked to him. "She is nae one to be played with. It is best that ye keep away from her."

"What do ye think I will do? Defile her? She is a childhood friend."

"And a beautiful woman," Alexander countered. "Let us be honest. Ye are nae interested in more than conquest and she is one who has evaded ye."

Something akin to fire rose from his stomach up to his chest, when the heat reached his face, Knox gritted his teeth. "As I stated, I have no romantic interest in her."

"Tell that to yer face," Alexander snapped. "I love ye, cousin. And I know ye. And I ken ye bore quickly once the conquest is accomplished."

What did he feel? Was it true that if he managed to get Sencha to allow him to court her, he would get bored? Somehow, he knew it was quite the opposite, and the thought terrified him.

"I am considering sending guardsmen out to sea in bìrlinns to the neighboring isles to inform the local lairds about the killer."

"What?" Knox turned back to Alexander. "What did ye just say?"

His cousin gave him a curious look. "I said to be considering sending…"

"Out to sea," Knox interrupted. "We have to go back." He turned the horse around, urging it into a gallop. "He is at the first house we stopped at."

Alexander caught up and called over to him. "Why do ye think that?"

"Because I never mentioned anything about Kyle being a fisherman and the woman responded that perhaps he'd escaped by sea. Why would anyone think of that?"

THEY TETHERED THE horses a good distance away from the small house. Then Knox and Alexander walked the rest of the way, keeping to the trees and bushes they could hide behind. Knox signaled for Alexander to remain behind a tall bush as he rushed to a tree closer to the house.

Somehow he had to approach from the back and not be seen. He worried about Alexander, it was not a good thing to get the laird injured. Of course Alexander would scoff if Knox suggested that he remain outside.

With an eye on the back window, he crouched and ran to stand on the corner of the house that would be invisible to anyone peering out. A few moments later, Alexander did the same.

Alexander silently signaled for Knox to round the cottage. He would whistle when in place and they would enter from both sides.

Rounding the small cottage, Knox unsheathed his sword. Once the blade was in hand, his body tensed, ready for battle. At the same time his breathing slowed, without direction, his instincts persevering energy.

So much discord and so many battles in the last years that

his mental and physical worked as one without him having to take time to prepare.

Nearing the back door he waited until hearing a shrill whistle and at the same time both he and Alex each kicked in a door. Screams filled the air as the woman and man scrambled under the table dragging a small child with them.

Caught unaware, mouth agape and only a knife in hand, Kyle turned in a circle first to the back door and then to Alexander.

The man knew he wouldn't win, and his hand trembled when holding up the feeble weapon. No contest against trained warriors and swords. "I will kill them," he threatened, glancing toward the table.

Alexander shook his head. "It is ye who will die today."

When Kyle turned to look at him, Knox advanced and sliced at the hand holding the knife almost severing it from his arm. Kyle yelled as the knife fell to the floor, barely making a sound.

The man turned toward him. "I am owed a fair trial. Ye cannae prove I killed Fitz."

"Ye tried to kill me and the woman," Knox said in a calm voice. "I can prove that. I was there."

The man had the audacity to give him a triumphant look and turned to Alex "Laird, I felt threatened by him. I was defending myself." Seeming to realize he was bleeding profusely, he grabbed his hand and cradled it against his stomach.

"And the lass?" Knox asked, tired of talking to the idiot. "Ye felt threatened by her?"

Kyle hobbled toward him. "I will go willingly."

As he passed the table, his gaze moved toward it and quick as a rabbit, he tried to grab another knife with his left hand.

It was all Knox needed. Before the man could grab it, he thrust his sword into the man's stomach and yanked it upward.

Kyle stumbled backward; his eyes went wide then he looked down at the open wound. He tried to say something, but lost the battle and collapsed to the ground, his left hand against the wound, the other uselessly hanging at his side as he tried to help himself.

At the man falling to the ground, the woman under the table screamed and the child began to cry.

Both he and Alexander exchanged glances, neither wanting to be who would try to calm the people. His cousin lost the silent exchange. As laird it would be more appropriate that he be the one who spoke to them.

Knox went to the dying man and taking him by the feet drug him from the room. Behind him, Alexander spoke in a calm voice to the family, coaxing them from their hiding places and no doubt offering to send men to make any necessary repairs.

When Alexander walked out, Kyle was dead. Knox nudged the body with the toe of his boot. "What are we to do with it?"

"The man said he would bury him." His cousin looked down at the body. "I suppose we will never ken why he killed Fritz."

DESPITE THE SENSE of relief at removing the threat, Knox had a tightness in his stomach as they rode away. No matter how many battles, or how many times he'd had to kill someone, after everything settled the fact he'd taken a life was not easy to accept.

His cousin understood and gave him time to brood as they continued on their way home. After a long time, Alexander met his gaze.

"If ye didn't kill him, I would have. He was going to be put to death regardless, and I didn't want the spectacle of a public execution. Our clan has had enough of it."

Knox nodded. "I thought the same."

"No matter what I say, it will nae help ye go through whatever ye need to do. Each time we do our duty, it leaves something behind that we will always carry," Alexander told him.

"Sometimes I tire of it. If only we could have peace. But it seems that people can never be completely at rest. They allow anger, resentment, and jealousy to take over. So the battle never ends." Knox let out a weary sigh.

They continued in silence, as there was nothing else to be said. When a creek came into view, they rode to the water's edge. Knox dismounted and went to wash his face and hands of the dead man's blood, hoping to remove any evidence of what had occurred.

Then he walked into the chilled water and dunked into it, boots, clothes, and all. A calmness took over as the water cleansed more than his body.

When he walked out of the creek, his cousin stood by a tree, silently keeping watch. "Are ye ready to go home?"

CHAPTER NINE

L AST MEAL WAS smaller than usual as no hearings were held that day. Other than a small group of guards who kept watch, it was only the family, along with Sencha and her mother who remained at the keep.

Nala explained that everyone, including the laird had gone in search of Kyle. It was the last effort that would be put toward it. After they returned the patrols would be tasked with looking for him while out, but performing their normal tasks.

At the news, her mother was tense, obviously nervous at the idea of returning home and Sencha being at risk.

If she were to be honest, Sencha doubted the man would come looking for her. He was more worried with not being caught. Besides, they had Gordon and several farmhands who would ensure no one came there uninvited.

"Ye can stay as long as ye wish. There is nae hurry for ye to leave," Nala assured them.

"Mother, we should return home. I am sure we will be safe. Gordon will nae allow anyone to hurt us."

Her mother shook her head, a tear trailing down her cheek. "It is ye I worry about. He may wish revenge."

There was little to be said that would soothe her mother's fragile state. It was understandable. They'd just gone through her uncle's situation and her being attacked. It was a wonder her mother got out of bed.

"Very well, we will remain a few more days," Sencha said covering her mother's hand with hers.

SENCHA LAY IN bed listening to her mother's even breathing. She'd drank some herbal tea that had calmed her enough so she might fall asleep, and she was now resting. Sencha on the other hand was restless.

Turning to her side, she shifted in an attempt to find a comfortable position, then she rolled to her back. Finally, she gave up and sat up. When Cook had offered her some of the same tea her mother had sipped, she should have accepted it.

Thinking that there was some tea left in the kitchen Sencha slipped from her bed, grabbed a lantern by the door, and lit it.

Thankful for the lantern as the corridor and stairwell were dark, Sencha made her way through the great room toward the kitchen. The keep was eerily silent, which was not what she was used to. During the day there were always people about, and the din of conversations seem to emanate from every corner.

Bare feet on the cold stone floor made her lift to her toes as she hurried around a corner, hoping the floor would be warmer in the kitchen. When she neared the doorway she paused as there was a light coming from inside. She placed the lantern on the floor and walked slowly to the arched doorway.

On the table where the servants had their meals was a lantern and in a chair with his back to her was a man bent over a bowl eating.

She eyed the hearth noting a pot hung over the fire, probably what he ate. She didn't have to see his face to ken who it was.

"Knox?"

He lifted his head but didn't turn to her.

Sencha walked in and rounded the table to look at him. When he kept his gaze downcast, she hesitated, but then placed her hands on the back of the chair at the end of the table.

"Is something wrong? What happened?"

He let out a weary breath. "Ye dinnae have to worry yerself any longer. Kyle, is dead."

Another question died on her lips. She didn't need to ask him. It was obvious he'd been there, or perhaps it was he who had killed the man. Instead, Sencha went to him and placed her arms around his shoulders and her head against his. "Thank ye."

When he breathed again, it was as if he needed to hear the words.

"Sometimes," Knox began. "It is good to be reminded that good comes from evil."

Without thinking, she pressed a kiss to his temple. "Whatever the deed is that weighs heavily upon ye, I ken ye did it because it was yer duty. Yer purpose as a warrior. To protect the clan is a burden ye carry well."

"Yer words…" he hesitated. "Are like a balm to my spirit."

Sencha pulled out the chair next to his, hating to break contact with him. For she had to admit the admiration she had for him had grown into something stronger.

Needing to touch him, she leaned against him and placed a hand over his. "I remembered something that happened when I was a wee lass of about six or seven. My brother and I were playing on the seashore and I fell and cut my knees. Athol laughed and wandered away, while I sat on the shore, crying. This boy, the same age as my brother, came to me and helped me to stand. He used his tunic to dry my tears and then lifted me up and carried me to sit under a tree. When I continued to sniffle, he jumped around making sounds like a dog and pig until I laughed."

Knox huffed. "Ye were a pitiful sight that day."

"Ye could have walked away, the way Athol did, but ye didn't. Even then, ye were caring and strong. It is because ye care that ye defended me and the clan today."

He turned to her and cupped her face with his large rough hands. His eyes were stormy, his breathing hitched. Sencha ken he was going to kiss her and that she would allow it. More than anything, she needed to feel his mouth over hers.

When his lips pressed against hers, she leaned into him, returning the kiss and allowing his mouth to plunder hers. Greedily, she parted her lips to allow for his tongue to explore deeper. He tasted of ale. Her arms went around his neck, and he pulled her onto his lap. His hands sliding down her back pulling her against him as the kiss deepened.

Sencha dragged her fingers through his hair loving the feel of the soft waves threading past. When his mouth traveled from her mouth to her neck, a soft moan escaped.

Shivering from the sensations that were new and wonderful. Heat pulsed down her center and she panted in attempts to control her breathing as Knox's tongue traced circles on the side of her neck.

Clinging to his wide shoulders, she felt as if about to lose control. Knox cupped her breast kneading it and bringing an onslaught of pure need. Sencha wasn't sure what to do. In that moment she wanted nothing more than to feel his body against hers. She allowed her imagination free reign. This was not the time for logical thought.

Breaking the kiss, both were breathless. He pressed an almost chaste kiss to her lips and lifted her and placed her back onto the chair never breaking eye contact.

"Why are ye nae married? Ye are perfect." His voice was husky, breathless.

The question was meant as a compliment, but the way he'd phrased it broke her heart. Knox didn't see a future between them. Sencha struggled not to look disappointed. What had she expected that one moment between them would change him?

"The two men I have loved, my father and my brother left me. One when death claimed him, the other by choice. I dinnae see myself trusting fate enough," she replied. Mentally she added, and now the third man I love will also go away from me.

For a long moment, Knox studied her. "Ye will nae remain alone. Of that I am sure."

As frustrating as the conversation had become, Sencha didn't move away. He needed her there and for this one moment, she would be there for him, just like he'd been there for her that day by the shore.

"I am sure the women of the village will be knocking each other out of the way to be with the roguish clan hero," she teased, nudging his shoulder with hers.

"I best stay away from the village. I would nae wish for anyone to get hurt," Knox quipped with a soft smile that didn't reach his eyes.

"Sencha, I wish I could be the man for ye. I sincerely mean it. But I am nae one to ever settle. Ye understand that?"

She had to swallow past the lump in her throat. Had she been so transparent that he could see how strongly she felt? Probably because she was not used to feeling such strong emotions and had never been kissed or touched by a man until now.

"I ken Knox. I dinnae expect anything. We can remain friends."

Not wishing for him to see that she was on the verge of tears, Sencha pushed back and stood. "I best get what I came for. It is late, Mother may wake and be upset at not finding me there."

There was no tea left, so she walked out of the kitchen empty-handed. Even if she'd found the tea, it was doubtful that even herbs would help her sleep that night.

Her heart was broken in two, it would take more than herbs to curb the pain that replaced the wonderful sensations from just moments earlier.

CHAPTER TEN

CROSSING THE COURTYARD, Knox stalked toward the practice field. The archers would in all probability already be almost done with practice. It didn't matter to him, he felt more like swordplay that morning.

Sencha had not been at first meal. Not seeing her that morning had disappointed him. Despite what she'd said before leaving the kitchen, she'd been hurt. It had been a huge mistake to kiss her, to touch her.

The beautiful woman was much too worthy for him to have touched her so intimately. The smell of her sweet lavender had been like a siren call to his senses. Everything about her was irresistible perfection and he'd been powerless to stop himself.

Kissing Sencha was like nothing he'd ever experienced with any other woman. It was familiar and comforting. Not only that, but when her body pressed against his there had been a feeling of comfort. A sense of finding the elusive place he could call home.

The moment had been as wonderful as it was terrifying. What had that meant? What was it about Sencha that brought so many emotions?

"Whatever yer thinking. It must be serious," Hendry said, staring at him. "I have been standing here for a long moment and ye didnae see me."

Knox blinked and shook his head. "True. My mind was elsewhere."

His friend chuckled and murmured something under his breath. As much as Knox hated to ask, he was curious.

"What did ye say?"

Hendry hesitated then studied him for a long moment. "The last time I saw that look, it was when Alex realized he was in love. I would ask who she is, but I have a good idea."

Opening his mouth, Knox started to deny it, but the words would not come out. Taken aback at the realization that what Hendry said was true, he could not formulate a response. Finally his brain kicked in. "I am nae in love."

"So ye say," Hendry said walking toward the practice field. "Do ye want to spare?"

BY MIDDAY, KNOX was too tired to think. He welcomed the exhaustion from swordplay followed by archery practice.

At the well, he pulled the rope to lift the bucket and poured the water into another smaller bucket. Carrying the clean water, he went behind the stables and removed his clothes. Then he washed up and poured water over himself to rinse.

He'd brought clean clothes to change into and dressed as quickly as possible, the brisk wind making him shiver.

When Knox entered the house, the midday meal was being served, and he walked toward a table where the guards sat.

"Knox, sit with me," Anni materialized in front of him. "I am sitting over there with my brother." The village girl motioned to another table.

"I thank ye, but there are things I must discuss with my

cousin." Knox made it up on the spot, not wishing to give the lass any illusions that he would want to progress to the level of speaking with her brother.

She gave him a narrow look, obviously not happy, but then turned on her heel and walked off.

With no choice but to find his cousin, he groaned at seeing Alex sitting with Nala and his aunt at the same table as Sencha and her mother.

He'd say something in passing to his cousin and then sit with the guards.

When he walked to the table, Nala stood and hugged him. "We are so proud of ye," the beauty exclaimed. "Everyone will be able to sleep peacefully now."

Sencha's mother followed suit standing and taking his hand in both of hers. The woman looked to be on the verge of tears. "I appreciate what ye and Alexander did. I was so worried about my lass." The woman lifted to her toes and pressed a kiss to his jaw and then motioned for Sencha to do the same. "Have ye thanked Knox properly lass?"

When her cheeks turned pink, she never looked more beautiful, and Knox couldn't keep from smiling.

Eyes moving away from his face, Sencha got up and walked toward him. Like her mother, she lifted to her toes and kissed his cheek. Knox almost closed his eyes but managed to keep a pleasant expression.

"Not only did ye find Kyle, but ye helped exonerate my uncle. It is much appreciated," Sencha said and quickly turned away.

Nala and Alex exchanged looks making him wonder if they suspected something had occurred between them. He chided himself, no one knew anything, and he would keep it that way.

"I was only performing my duty," Knox heard himself say. "Alex, if ye dinnae require anything else from me, I will retire early."

His cousin's eyes traveled from Sencha to him. "Not until the morning. Take a guard and escort Sencha and her mother home. Walk through the house and around it to ensure nothing has been tampered with."

"It is nae required. I am sure we are safe now. Gordon can take us," Sencha protested.

Her mother gave her a look and she stopped speaking. "Gordon is nae here. We would appreciate it so very much. It will set my mind at ease."

Knox met Sencha's gaze for a moment, and she swallowed visibly, her eyes flying to the others at the table as if expecting they would guess what had occurred between them.

"After first meal?" he asked Sencha's mother who nodded.

"Aye, we will be ready."

SENCHA AND NALA were finally able to have time alone. They'd gone to the sitting room on the same floor as the bedchambers to sit and talk.

Nala lifted a basket of embroidery and threads and moved things around in search of whatever she needed to use next.

"I am so glad all has been cleared up and yer uncle is free to return to his life," Nala said lifting an embroidered cloth studying it.

"The poor man was terrified. I believe it will be a long time before he recovers," Sencha replied sipping from her glass of honeyed mead.

Just then the door opened, and Alexander entered. Although he gave Sencha a brief nod, his attention was fully on Nala. He neared and placed a kiss to his wife's temple. "How fare ye?"

Her friend seemed to glow with happiness as she looked at her husband. "So much better knowing the danger of my dearest friend being harmed is over."

The laird nodded. "I regret what yer family had to endure, Sencha." He met her eyes. "Sometimes circumstances lead in the wrong direction."

"I understand, and so do my aunt and uncle. It was true that he went to the fishing village and carried a knife which made it easy for him to be blamed."

After a brush of his lips over Nala's he left with a promise to take her for a walk later.

Sencha studied the door through which the man had walked. "How does it feel to be in love?"

"Both wonderful and terrifying," Nala replied. "I cannae imagine my life without Alex. When I'm near him, my heart soars. I never thought feelings like these existed."

"I cannae imagine." Sencha let out a long slow breath. "It is lovely to witness interactions between the both of ye."

"Ye will be in love soon and will ken how special and rare it is." Nala gave her a pointed look. "Allow yerself to feel freely dear friend."

"Ha," Sencha replied. "If I remember correctly, both ye and Alex were not keen on the idea of falling in love."

Nala laughed. "Very true. I am so glad not to have allowed fear to keep me from being honest with myself."

She managed to turn the conversation to plans for other

visits when suddenly Nala held up a hand. "I must ask. What about Knox? Have ye considered him? It is obvious ye and he are attracted to one another."

"The man is a rogue, through and through. Do ye really expect he will settle anytime soon?" Sencha shook her head. "Caring for a man like him will only lead to heartbreak."

"Is that ye or fear who speaks?"

As much as she wanted to ignore Nala's comment, Sencha had to consider the question. "I dinnae ken."

MORNING CAME, AND both she and her mother went to the great room for first meal. Sencha did her best not to look for Knox, but it was as if her eyes had a mind of their own and scanned the room until they found him.

He sat at the high board next to the laird, seeming to be in a serious conversation by the lowering of their brows. As if sensing her perusal, Knox's eyes lifted and met hers and then lowered. It was but a glance and still her entire body hummed with awareness.

The sooner they returned home, and she was away from him, the better. All night she'd relived the kiss they'd shared. The way it felt to have his lips over hers and his hard muscular body against hers. The feel of his hands on her waist and cupping her breast. No matter how much she wanted to forget the experience, at the same time, it was something she wished to keep in the forefront of her memory. As hurtful as it was that he didnae feel as strongly for her, she suspected no other man would ever make her feel like he did.

In that brief encounter, it had been only him and her and nothing else. The entire world—all the people in it and all their worries—had disappeared. The air had surrounded them like a cloak, blocking everything else out. Just the sights, sounds, and smells of their intimacy were all she could remember, and it was something she would treasure forever.

"Sencha dinnae forget, ye promised to come and visit in a sennight," Nala reminded her as soon as they sat. "We will have a picnic."

"It will be too cold for a picnic," her mother stated. "Unless ye wish to catch yer death, I think ye should remain indoors."

Nala pouted. "The weather has been so temperate I had nae considered that. I will have to plan something else just as fun." Her face brightened. "A bonfire dance," she exclaimed clapping her hands.

"Splendid idea," the laird's mother professed. "A perfect opportunity for couples to court for marriage."

Everyone turned to look at Sencha and she pretended a sudden intent interest in the food on her plate.

"Sencha, it is past yer time to marry," her mother said a bit too loudly. Several men nearby cleared their throats.

"I do believe ye are scaring those nearby," Sencha replied, giving her mother a warm look. "Besides, if someone wanted to court me, they would have by now."

Nala, who was becoming much too animated, huffed. "I believe the reason ye remain unattached is because ye never leave yer house. Other than to visit me and once every other month ye go to the village. Otherwise, ye are never seen."

"Should we speak about something else?" Sencha suggested.

The laird's mother didn't take heed. "We must make sure all the unattached women from surrounding areas are invited, there are many single guardsmen that require a wife."

A couple of men coughed, one sounded as if he was choking.

Nala glared in their direction. "Dinnae try to come up with excuses not to attend the bonfire dance," she said toward the table where guards sat pretending not to hear. "I am talking to ye, Liam, Caleb, Tom, and Hendry."

They all replied, "We will be present, my lady."

"Good," Nala said with a satisfied look then returned her attention to Sencha. "We must discuss who ye find to yer liking and what ye wish for."

"I wish for a hole to appear and swallow me alive," Sencha replied and despite attempting to give her a stern look, her mother laughed.

"The Grants should be invited," her mother suggested. "Their lands are near ours and any marriage would mean Sencha could remain nearby."

Nala looked over to Sencha who mouthed *no* and shook her head. Her friend's smile stretched across her face. "I will see to it."

With that, the conversation changed to a discussion about what food should be prepared and Sencha was glad to be left alone to consider how she could pretend to be too ill to attend.

THEY SET OFF for home before midday as the trip would take a pair of hours. Sencha settled into the coach and her mother sat next to her and peered out the opening. "Knox has mounted," her mother stated the obvious. "The other guard I believe is called Liam. He is a handsome man, have ye spoken to him?"

"Aye, many times. It was obvious he didnae find me in the least bit interesting." Sencha had only spoken to the man once, and she made up the second part.

They rode for a while discussing other things. Then, of course, her mother brought up the bonfire and Sencha admitted to not wishing to go.

"Do ye not wish to marry, but remain alone for the rest of yer life?" Her mother gave her a pointed look. "Honestly Sencha, I dinnae understand ye. What is it? Explain it to me."

Sencha let out a breath. "Men dinane stay. I ken Father dinnae leave us purposely, but he died so long ago and ye still remain alone. Then there's Athos. He would rather travel the world than to look after us properly."

Her mother covered her hand with hers. "It is nae always like that my darling. Look at Nala's parents, they have been married for a long time and are happy. Then there's yer aunt Jane and uncle Donald. Even though yer father died, I am so grateful for the years we had together."

"How do I ken who the right man is? What feelings should I trust?"

The carriage came to a stop, and both fell silent. The door opened and Knox peered in. "One of the horses is limping. He may have a stone caught in his hoof."

"We will stretch our legs then," her mother said standing and holding out her hand for him to help her out. Sencha followed suit, not holding out her hand. She let out a squeak of surprise when Knox took her by the waist and lowered her to the ground.

Her face reddened, but she kept her attention on the

ground and hurried toward the side of the road. Her mother was studying a patch of what looked to be weeds and then bent to study them closer. "I believe this is feverfew, see about getting something to dig it out by the roots dear."

Sencha gave her mother an incredulous look. "What exactly do ye think I can find to undergo such a task?"

"Ask Knox for his dagger." Her mother made shooing motions with her hands and continued to search further.

Trudging back to the carriage, Sencha approached Knox who watched the other guard inspecting the horse's front hoof. "I need to borrow yer dagger."

With a pinched brow he turned to her. "Who do ye plan to stab?"

"Mother wishes for me to dig up a plant by the roots."

His eyebrows shot up. His eyes widened. His hand went to the blade at his hip. "With my dagger?" Obviously he found the thought of his blade going into the dirt offensive.

For some reason, Sencha found it amusing and she held out her hand. "Dagger please."

Rounding her, he went to his horse and from a saddlebag, pulled out a small spade. "This would better serve ye."

She eyed him. "Why do ye carry this?"

"There are many times it is required, especially when one has to spend days outdoors."

Understanding and not wishing for a more elaborate explanation Sencha reached for it.

"Ye act differently toward me as of late." His gold speckled eyes met hers and she almost lost her ability to breathe. "I wish things could be different between us."

It took a great deal of willpower, but somehow she managed not to kick him. The statement was ridiculous since it was he that ensured she understood he had no plans to settle. At least not with her.

Instead of replying, she took the small spade and went to find her mother, who was pointing at another plant. "Sage," she said by way of explanation. "This is a most fortuitous stop," she added with a firm nod.

IT WAS LATE afternoon when they arrived at Sencha's home. Before Knox could help her out, Sencha pushed the carriage door open and scrambled down. Using the excuse of putting the surprisingly still thriving plants into the ground she hurried away.

The small garden outside the kitchen was a bit overrun with weeds. The task would give her something to do for the next few days. A good distraction, Sencha considered. From a line of pots with only dirt inside Sencha got two and placed them onto a bench.

Voices of the others, including Gordon who'd come to greet the carriage carried over.

"Ye were to wait until we ensure the surroundings were safe," Knox said striding into the garden.

Sencha didn't bother to straighten from digging into the dirt with her hands and gently putting the new plants into place ensuring not to bruise the roots. "I am sure if anything was amiss, the farmhands would have rushed to inform us."

"I like this place and have often considered building a home like it on my land." Knox's statement had a tinge of wistfulness.

"Why do ye nae do it?" Sencha asked her attention on the

second plant.

"Living alone does nae appeal to me now. When I am older and no longer a guard, I will do it."

Sencha looked up to him. "Living alone when older seems a sad existence."

Their eyes held for a long moment, and it was Sencha who looked away first. "I would nae wish to grow old alone."

Liam rounded the corner and stopped at seeing them. "Everything is well. We have been invited to remain for a meal." He glanced to Sencha. "Yer mother is very kind."

Sencha smiled at Liam. "Aye, she is. Beware, she is on the hunt to find me a husband."

"I dinnae mind," Liam replied with a crooked grin.

When Knox's eyes narrowed, she pretended not to notice.

"Ye say that now," Sencha teased back rounding Knox and walking to Liam. "I will show ye were ye can wash up and then help Mother make something for the meal."

CHAPTER ELEVEN

T HE WOODS SURROUNDING Ailith's cottage served to keep the wind at bay. Hendry pulled his horse to a stop a short distance away and studied the small home.

Smoke wafted from the chimney, and he imagined the woman was inside either cooking or keeping the fire going to stay warm.

As a leader he could have sent a guard to inform the widow that the danger of an attack was gone, but he'd felt compelled to come himself.

Riding closer, he dismounted and tethered his horse to a young tree and walked to the front door.

Immediately barking from inside sounded reminding him of Ailith's faithful and very protective companion. It was smart of her to have the dog, it would certainly deter someone from attempting to enter and steal or cause harm.

A curtain shifted and she looked out, at recognizing him, she moved from the window and moments later the door opened.

"Ye can come in." The invitation came as a surprise. She pulled the door open with one hand and held her dog back with the other hand. "Teller will nae bite ye if I invite ye in."

By the baring of his teeth, Hendry wasn't assured, but he walked in.

Ailith went to a chair that had blankets on it and lowered into it. Her face was flushed and nose was red. It explained why she wouldn't go outside.

"Ye are ill," Hendry commented while studying her. "How long have ye been unwell?"

She waved away his concern. "Only since yesterday. I am sure I will be much better in a day or two."

There wasn't a pot on the hook by the hearth. Or evidence of any meal having been eaten. No dirt bowls or cups to be found.

Finding the kettle empty as well, he got a bucket and went back out. The dog, probably needing to relieve itself, followed him out and upon Hendry filling the bucket from the well, he trotted beside him back inside.

"What are ye doing?" Ailith asked as he filled the kettle and brought it to the hearth, once he hung it over the waning fire, he added a log.

"Ye need to eat and drink something." He looked across to the table to where there was a basket with potatoes and carrots beside a piece of salted meat on a plate.

While the water in the kettle heated, he went about peeling and chopping the vegetables and meat and placed them into a small pot that he also filled with water.

Ailith had fallen asleep by the time he replaced the kettle with the pot over the fire. The woman didnae feel well in the least, otherwise, she would have protested more.

He placed chopped herbs into a cup and added the boiling water, allowing them to seep.

The dog settled on the floor next to his mistress, despite his being invited in, the animal didnae trust him fully. It was a good thing.

"Ailith," he said in a loud but calm voice. "Drink this." Hendry held out the cup with a green tinged liquid inside.

Her eyes opened and then widened as she seem to realize she'd fallen asleep. "I-I am fine, ye dinnae have to…" She took the cup not finishing her sentence, seeming to realize that yes, she did need his help. Not only that, but the pot over the fire was now filling the space with a wonderful aroma of stew.

While she drank, he lowered to the only other chair in the room and kept an eye on her. "I can take ye to the keep. Ye can recover there."

The keep was the last place the woman would wish to go, so Hendry added, "Or to the village. Do ye ken someone there?"

Ailith considered what he said, her gaze meeting his for a beat before she looked away. "I would be grateful if ye can send a message to my sister Helena. I am sure she will come with her husband to see about me."

"Very well," Hendry said and waited in silence as she finished the herbal water. "I am nae sure what I boiled, I assume ye picked it for yer ailment."

She nodded. "Aye."

When the stew was done, Ailith went to the table and looked on as he ladled it into a bowl for her. Then waited as he placed a smaller amount into a bowl for himself and then placed some into a flat plate for the dog.

They ate in silence, the only sound was moments later when he placed the cooled food on the floor for the dog, who gobbled it up.

"I do appreciate this," Ailith said in a soft voice. "I was

planning to cook, but I found it hard to motivate myself to do it. Poor Teller has been eating bread since the day before yesterday."

Hendry realized she must have gotten ill right after he'd seen her last. "Why do ye nae move to live in the village? It is nae safe to be out here alone."

Ailith looked about the cottage, and by the forlorn expression, Hendry knew she thought of her dead husband. "I have considered it."

Once she finished, Hendry went to the well to wash the dirty dishes, then filled the bucket and brought fresh water back inside. After the leftover stew was properly covered with a small cloth and he ensured the kettle was filled and hung by the hearth did he feel more at ease leaving the woman alone.

"I will send someone with the message to yer sister and return to see about ye the day after tomorrow," he told her. "If yer sister is nae here, I will take ye to the village myself."

By the changes in expression, Ailith considered what to say. "She will come. I am sure of it."

Hendry walked out, pulling the door closed behind him.

Once mounted he studied the front of the cottage. Something had changed between himself and Ailith.

Something akin to hope flickered in his chest.

CHAPTER TWELVE

"WE MUST PREPARE for the bonfire," Sencha's mother announced that morning as they sat down to break their fast. "It takes place tomorrow, so I have asked Gordon to take us to the keep this afternoon."

By her mother's expression, she was excited for the outing. Sencha narrowed her eyes. "Is Gordon attending with us?"

"Yes, he is." Her mother's cheeks pinkened and joy flared in Sencha.

"I am glad," Sencha replied. "That way we can leave the following morning."

A trickle of sunlight came through the window casting lines of light across the table where they sat. Sencha followed the path of the rays to the floor to find her dog stretched out snoring lightly.

"It is the most perfect of mornings. I dinnae wish to spoil it by stating this, but I implore ye Mother, dinnae play matchmaker. If I find a man to my liking, I will let ye know, but I dinnae require yer assistance."

Her mother gave her a pointed look. "If that were true, ye would be wedded by now. Ye do require help Sencha. We will remain at the keep for a day after the bonfire, to ensure that if there is a man interested, ye have time to be available."

There was something afoot, Sencha was sure of it. Obviously her mother had formulated a plan, and it meant she'd have to be extra vigilant.

"Mother, is there someone ye would pick for me?" She hoped to gain insight and a hint as to whom her mother would be pushing in her direction.

"Oh, I dinnae ken. There are plenty of eligible men at the keep, most of them are part of the guard, which means they have a steady flow of coin. If the Grants attend, one of the sons would be a good match for ye." Her mother tapped a forefinger to her chin. "Then there is Knox, my opinion of him has shifted. He fought tirelessly to defend yer uncle. And not once did I see him in the company of a woman whilst we visited."

"I did," Sencha said, unsure why she'd blurted it out. "That woman, Anni was constantly hanging on his arm."

Her mother waved as hand dismissing the fact. "It is a shame that lass is so desperate to find a husband that she makes a fool of herself. I wish someone would marry the poor thing. It was obvious Knox was nae interested."

It hadn't been as obvious to Sencha, but she kept the remark to herself. So it seemed her mother didn't exactly have someone specific in mind. Good.

A DAY LATER when the bonfire festivities began, Sencha was excited at the prospect of music and dance. So far she'd managed to avoid Knox, and she hoped to keep it that way. Being away had helped her push any feelings for him aside, but that didn't mean she wanted to spend time with him unnecessarily. This night she planned to enjoy herself and perhaps dance with Liam, or maybe even Hendry. Admittedly, most of their interactions had been more friendly than flirtatious, but at the same time, she was comfortable around them. There was always time for them to have more interactions and perhaps it could become more than just friendly between them.

The huge bonfire was lit just outside the gates in the middle of an open field. Chairs and benches were scattered about to provide places to sit for those attending.

Over a smaller fire nearby a pig cooked, and already pieces were being sliced off and served along with chunks of appetizing bread.

With her food in hand, Sencha wandered through the people gathered looking for her mother or someone to sit with.

"Sencha!" Nala called out from where she and several others sat perched on wooden chairs with shawls over their shoulders. The light and heat from the bonfire made it so that they didn't require cloaks or heavy blankets.

"Where is my mother?" Sencha asked looking around.

Ainslie pointed to a group of older people, which included her mother and Gordon. "She is over there."

Just as she sat, a trio of fiddlers began playing a lively tune. Immediately people jumped up from where they sat or strode in from where they'd been standing and began dancing. As the dancers moved to the music, others clapped joining in the moment.

Sencha ate her meal, moaning at the taste of the succulent meat. "This is so good. Did ye eat?" she asked Nala who nodded.

"Aye, twice," her friend replied. "Hurry and finish so we

can dance."

"Go ahead," Sencha replied. "I will join ye in a minute." She took another bite, not wishing to waste a single morsel.

Moments later, she licked her fingers and sighed happily.

Lowering to sit next to her, Knox settled into the chair Nala had vacated. At once her heartbeat accelerated and her breath caught. How could just his mere presence affect her so? Sencha refused to look at him, keeping her attention on the dancers.

She considered standing and going to join Nala but decided not to let him feel as if he mattered so much as to get a reaction from her.

"I have nae spoken to ye since ye arrived," he commented, looking at her. "Have ye been avoiding me?"

Sencha looked to the fire before replying. "Why would I do that? If our paths have nae crossed it is nae because I have done anything."

The corners of his lips twitched taking her attention. To her consternation, the reminder of those very same lips being against hers slammed into her mind.

"Ye seem well recovered," Knox said studying her face. "Just as beautiful as ever."

Taken aback at the compliment, Sencha was speechless. She turned her attention back to the fire.

A new song began, and Knox reached for her hand. "Dance with me?" He stood and pulled her to her feet.

The fact she became mute, and all thought left her head at his touch was as surprising as it was annoying.

She allowed him to lead her to join the other dancers and they began moving in time with the music, which required them to hold hands and turn in a circle. Then they changed partners and repeated the same dance.

After changing partners several times, Sencha was enjoying the dance. When she returned to Knox, he gripped her hands once again as they whirled. Both of them grinning widely.

They began another rotation as the music continued. It was a fun dance; she had to admit.

By the time the song ended she was once again partnered with Knox and too breathless to speak as he guided her away from the dancing.

Allowing him to lead her, it was a few moments before she noticed they were far away from the others. Sencha looked up. "The fresh air feels good after being so close to the fire," she said realizing why he'd led her there.

"It is a nice night," Knox replied, his eyes moving from her face toward the fire.

"Has yer mother found a man to marry ye?" Knox studied her face, obviously waiting for her to reply.

A sense that he hoped she would agree made her want to roll her eyes. "She is allowing me to inform her when I find someone suitable." She leaned on a short wall, needing to put space between them.

"And have ye?" He took a step closer.

"I think Liam would be a good match for me. I enjoy his company."

Knox's eyes narrowed. "Company? Ye and he have spent time together then?" From the intent way he studied her, Sencha wasn't sure if he was angry or just very interested in her reply.

"Is there any reason he would nae be a suitable match? Is

he interested in someone?" Sencha asked genuinely wishing to ken. More than anything, she wanted Knox to suggest himself, but she understood it would never happen.

Slowly he shook his head. "Liam is a good man. That I ken of he is not courting anyone."

The answer should have been satisfying. Should have made her happy. Instead it felt flat. But she smiled to hide the fact it mattered little. "That is good news."

"We best return before Mother searches for me." Sencha turned away only to stop when Knox took her upper arm.

Pivoting toward him, she knew she was on the brink of losing the fight and telling him it was he who she wanted. Telling him she would wait for him and not think of marriage to anyone else. Instead, she bit her bottom lip. As if by mutual agreement, they came together, their mouths meeting, their bodies colliding. Softness against solid, hands on each other, every sense overridden by desire. She could neither hear, smell, taste, not touch anything other than the man who held her in a possessive embrace, claiming her as his.

In that moment while he feasted on her mouth, their breathing intermingled, she was his, only his.

Her back to the wall, Sencha was trapped in his wonderful embrace, and she realized ownership of her body, mind, and soul belonged to Knox. He sought to touch every part of her, his hands sliding down her back, cupping her bottom, and pulling her against his arousal.

Sencha wrapped her arms around his neck with need like she'd never felt before, she pushed into him, lifting her leg and curling it around his waist. The fire inside her had to be sated, and she didn't care how.

Taking her mouth anew, Knox lifted her skirts and glided his hand, fingers trailing up her leg to her inner thigh.

"Let me pleasure ye, give ye release." His breathless words caressed her ear.

Clinging to his shoulders, Sencha nodded. "Aye. Please."

As he trailed his tongue down the side of her throat to the top of her breasts, his hand traveled to between her legs and his fingers slid down the center of her sex.

Tingles of awareness shot through her, and she gasped. Whatever he did, she needed more, and she moaned loudly overwhelmed with each caress.

In the back of her mind, she wondered if he was ruining her for another man, if she was losing herself wholly to him.

It could be that she stiffened because Knox whispered into her ear, "Ye will remain a maiden."

At the same time, he began to stroke something magical, and the most wonderful sensations were causing her to forget everything. He continued the motions over and over until Sencha exploded with so much force, she cried out. Thankfully, Knox covered her mouth with his swallowing the sounds she made.

Sencha found herself breathless once again. Although this time was very different from losing her breath from dancing, Sencha clung to him as he lowered her leg and smoothed her skirts. His chest rose and fell as he pulled her against him, his hand cradling her head as if she were the most precious of things.

"We have lingered away too long. We must return." Sencha went to take a step away, but her legs felt like weak as a newborn doe.

Knox pressed a kiss to her lips. "I am nae sure to be able to…"

"Dinnae finish that sentence. Dinna ruin this experience for me." Sencha found that her legs regained their strength, and she took another step away.

"Wait," Knox held her hand. "Sencha, can we speak tomorrow?"

She nodded and hurried away, forgetting that her shawl remained on the ground next to the wall.

SENCHA SAT UP with a start, she'd overslept. Looking over to her mother's bed, she noticed it was empty. The first thought that came was what had occurred between her and Knox the night before. At recalling the intimacy of the moment, heat crept up from her stomach to her face. How could she possibly show her face? Faking feeling unwell was probably the best thing to do that day and remain in the room until it was time to leave.

Just then the door opened, and her mother walked in, seeming breathless and somewhat flustered.

"What happened Mother?" Sencha went to her. "Is something wrong?"

"I am marrying Gordon," her mother blurted. "Last night, he asked. Today, the vicar comes, and our marriage ceremony will take place here in the chapel."

Sencha threw her arms around her mother, and they circled, both laughing. "I am so glad. It took ye both long enough," Sencha said pressing a kiss to her mother's cheek.

"Why is the ceremony so soon? Why here?"

Despite being happy for her mother, it seemed the marriage would mean she would remain at the keep at least another day.

"We spoke about it with Alexander, and he suggested it. Honestly there is nae a need to wait. We are nae young and have known each other for years. I dinnae wish to linger here overly long."

Her mother helped her to dress. "I need ye to go to the house and retrieve my green dress, ye ken the one I wore for Nala's wedding. Nala suggested that ye borrow a dress from her, but it is up to ye."

Trying to keep track of the tasks, Sencha nodded, and her mother prattled on. "Bring enough clothes so that ye can remain here for another pair of days."

Sencha pulled the strings of her skirt and tied them. "Why will I stay here? Can I not go home with ye and Gordon..." She stopped. "Never mind. Aye, of course I will stay."

It was wonderful to see her mother's face bright with excitement and as they walked from the room, Sencha turned for her shawl. "Mother, did ye take my shawl?"

Her mother shook her head. "I have nae seen it."

CHAPTER THIRTEEN

"**H**OLD. RELEASE!" KNOX called out to the archers. It was a windy day, perfect for practicing how to adjust their stance and aim. The men took two steps closer to their targets and stopped, he called out the commands again.

A guard walked toward him and stood to the side. "An escort will be required to take Miss Sencha home and bring her back promptly. It is to be a fast trip."

"I will go," Knox stated, not giving the man a chance to ask if he could be the one to accompany Sencha. "Why the hurry?"

"There is to be a marriage this evening. I dinnae ken if it is her or someone else. In all probability her." The guard stalked away, obviously annoyed that he was not going to have a day away from guard duties.

Who was Sencha to marry in such a rush? It made little sense. Had her mother discovered what had occurred between them and demanded it? Obviously she'd named someone to marry that wasn't him, else he would've been called in to explain.

Finding his hands were curled into fists, Knox released a breath through flared nostrils. "If anyone was to marry the lass, it had to be him. After all, he was who'd been with her the night before.

Storming into the great room, the first thing he noticed

were the women all gathered at a table speaking excitedly. He narrowed his eyes in their direction. Sencha must have sensed him because she looked toward him and quickly away.

He proceeded across the room to where Alex was and lowered to the chair next to him. "I hear there is to be a wedding."

Doing his best to unclench his jaw, he waited for the reply.

"Oh, aye, tonight. Who is to escort Sencha to get her and her mother's dresses?"

"Why the hurry?"

Alex looked toward the group of women and then scanned the room. "It is a good match. Both are anxious."

Nothing made sense and all he could do was look to find Sencha gathering a small satchel and preparing to leave.

"I will take her," he informed Alexander and then walked to catch up with Sencha who headed for the door.

Without a backward glance, she hurried to the waiting carriage and climbed in. Knox signaled to the driver and climbed in after her.

Just as he sat, the carriage began moving and Sencha's wide eyes met his. "Wh-what are ye doing?"

"We must speak."

She pulled a cloak around herself tightly her eyes looking to the door as if she considered jumping out. "I lost my shawl."

Knox blinked unsure why she thought to say it. "I found it. It's in the entryway on the side table."

"Oh." She looked out the window. "I don't understand why ye are here... in the carriage... with me."

He cleared his throat. "Because we must speak."

"There is nothing to discuss. I understand yer stance on

marriage and commitment. Ye dinnae wish for the burden of a wife or family. Ye dinnae owe me anything. What occurred between us, however enjoyable, must never happen again."

This time it was Knox who looked out the window, his mind in a jumble. Would he stand back and allow another man to marry her? Why did the thought of her with another make him want to kill whomever it was?"

He cleared his throat. "This marriage. It is quite abrupt."

Her eyes slid to him. "Aye, it is, but I am glad for it." Her lips curved. "Admittedly, when I first suggested it, I was unsure it would happen."

This time his throat almost closed and he coughed. "Ye wish for it to be, then?"

"Of course. We cannae stand about and wait for things. Life continues and we grow older. It is much better to be happy than alone. Seeing my mother so happy makes me happy as well."

"So yer mother... she is glad for it then?"

"She is." Sencha frowned. "Why are ye so interested in this?"

This was it. He had to decide. He would either fight for her or forever lose Sencha to another. His gut clenched and mouth went dry. As a warrior he was accustomed to fear, but this moment made his blood run cold. He had a pair of hours to convince the woman in front of him that he was in love with her and would not accept that she marry anyone but him.

"Ye will marry me, nae anyone else."

Sencha opened her mouth, but he continued speaking. Before hearing any other utterings about who this man was, he had to plead his case.

"I find the idea of ye marrying another unfathomable. There is and will forever be only one woman for me. It is ye, Sencha. Aye, it scares me, the idea of marriage, but ye marrying another is a much greater fear. I dinnae ken who this man is, but I am willing to wager, he will never make ye feel the things ye feel with me."

He expected Sencha to be shocked by his declaration, but the silence stretched for far longer than he'd hoped. She stared at him with an unreadable expression, something between surprise and confusion. Then she began to laugh.

Sencha laughed so much, she had to wipe tears from her eyes. She'd stop, look at him and fall into new bouts of mirth. Sencha laughed until she held both arms around her mid-section.

"It hurts…oh, goodness. My stomach…" Again she began laughing falling sideways breathless.

Finally sobering, she straightened, her face pink from the laughter.

"What do ye find so funny about what I said?" Knox was hurt and angry at her reaction.

"Dinnae be cross with me." Sencha held her stomach and let out a breath. "I have nae laughed this hard in a long time."

"Ye dinnae have to worry about having to marry me. It is my mother who is getting married to Gordon. Not me."

"I thought it was ye," Knox admitted, now realizing why his declaration made Sencha laugh. At the same time, it was his true feelings and that she'd not taken his sentiments seriously was concerning.

"Knox." The way she said his name was like a caress. "Did ye really mean what ye said?"

He nodded. "Ye dinnae feel the same, I gather." When he looked at her, Sencha remained stock-still, her teeth sinking into her bottom lip, and her brows lowered.

"I feel exactly the same, of course I do. I have for a long time," she finally uttered.

A strange feeling like that of a burden taken from his shoulders made him feel lighter. At the same time, he was tongue-tied, unsure what to say.

"Would ye have professed how ye feel if circumstances had nae pushed ye to it?" Sencha asked in a low uncertain voice.

It was best to answer honestly. "My feelings have grown stronger for ye. After last night, I could nae stop thinking about ye. When I found yer shawl, I kept it with me, it was as if a part of ye remained with me through the night."

Now he'd admitted to sleeping with her shawl. What would he do next, write poetry? Knox bit back on his molars. "I mean, until I placed it on the side table." Despite his pledge of honesty, a man could only admit to so much.

There was a slight lift to the corners of her mouth. She let out a breath. "Ye didnae answer my question. It leads me to believe ye would have held back yer declaration."

"What I said I meant. I do wish for ye to be mine."

Her right brow arched as she met his gaze. "I am nae sure ye have changed yer ways. I have seen that village girl hanging about ye almost daily. Ye must consider if ye are truly ready to marry. To be with only one woman."

Knox was struck silent as in truth, the idea of settling was a bit terrifying.

Leaning forward, Sencha gave him a knowing look. "Unlike ye, I have decided it is time that I find a suitable husband.

As much as it pains me, I wish to marry a man who is sure. Nae one who is scared of the idea of marriage."

Although he'd heard her words, his attention was taken fully by her proximity and the smell of sweet lavender that seemed to cling to her. Everything a reminder of how she'd come undone in his arms, how she'd tasted, and the sounds of her husky moans when he'd taken her to release.

"Knox," she said getting his attention. "It seems we have arrived."

IT WAS BUT a matter of moments before Sencha returned from inside the house with her mother's dress and the other items they required.

Knox had walked away to a nearby corral and studied the horses within. The animals were of good breeding stock as her brother had purchased them on one of his meanderings through Scotland.

SENCHA STUDIED KNOX. Of course he was deep in thought and the fact that it was not an easy decision to be with her, broke Sencha's heart. To her, it was obvious the man was not ready to be a husband and start a family.

Despite her deep feelings for him, she was not going to be someone a man settled for whilst wishing for his old life. Although she had no doubt that Knox would be loyal and faithful to her, over time he would resent losing his freedom.

On the way back to the keep, Sencha closed her eyes, hoping to sleep and avoid any further discussions with Knox. Once they arrived at the keep, she would make more of an effort with either Liam or Hendry. It could be one of them was ready to find a wife. Both were handsome in different ways. Liam was well-built, yet slender, with the build of an agile fighter. Hendry was quite handsome and broad-shouldered, with a cleft on his chin. Both were leaders in the guard and more importantly, her mother liked them.

"Sencha," Knox nudged her, and her eyes flew open. She'd actually fallen asleep.

"Aye? What is it?"

"Yer neck was at an alarming angle, ye would be quite sore for the rest of the day." He leaned close and placed a folded item against the side of the carriage so she could rest upon it. Then his eyes met hers. "There that is better."

Leaning on the folded item that was either her shawl or perhaps an item from her mother's wardrobe, she gave him a grateful smile.

With him so close, it was hard to keep from leaning closer and pressing a kiss to his lips. It would be a horrible mistake. The worst thing she could do.

Her eyes locked on his lips, she found it impossible to look away. Sencha almost sagged with relief when his mouth covered hers.

Her mind reeled with the many reasons she should stop the kiss, but her body paid no heed as she wrapped her arms around his neck and pulled him closer.

They broke away, both breathless and Sencha pushed him back. "I cannae marry ye. Ye are nae ready."

Knox sat back and crossed his arms over his chest, with a stony expression. "I am glad ye ken me so well," he said dryly.

Thankfully moments later the carriage came to a stop as they'd arrived at the keep.

CHAPTER FOURTEEN

L AST MEAL WAS lively. Her mother's marriage ceremony had been heartwarming with only a few in attendance. The Ross family, her aunt and uncle, and Nala's parents.

Once they ate, the newlywed couple left to begin their new life together. Sencha had hugged her mother tightly as tears of happiness trickled down both their cheeks.

"Now ye will have to find a husband, so ye can begin a family and life of yer own," her aunt Jane said motioning about the room. "There are plenty of choices here."

Her uncle winked at her. "Aye, I think ye have caught several pairs of eyes."

Heat crept up to her cheeks and she covered them with both hands. "I cannae just conjure a husband."

Everyone laughed and despite the fact Knox had not disagreed with her earlier, she found herself enjoying the evening.

Joining Nala and several others in a lively dance, Sencha was surprised when after men joined, Liam came to partner with her.

By the time the jig ended, she was breathless and flushed. "Would ye like to go outside for fresh air?" Liam asked.

It was a harmless ask, but Sencha hesitated. What if he tried to kiss her? Was she ready for it?

"Aye, that would be lovely," she heard herself reply.

It was cool outside, and it felt wonderful against her heated skin. Sencha walked to the edge of the walled in garden. "It is rather hot inside is it not?"

"It is," Liam replied walking closer. "I wish to ask ye something?"

"Of course," Sencha said, her gut clenching.

He gave her a curious look. "Ye seem panicked."

"I am nae." Doing her best to regain control of her racing heart and breath, Sencha let out a giggle, that indeed sounded as if she was on the verge of a scream.

"What I wish to ask ye," he began. "What are yer feelings toward Knox? There seems to be something between the two of ye. If that is so, then I will nae pursue ye for courting."

Was it so obvious that others had noticed? If she was to find a husband, would it be fair to the man if she was not honest? At the same time, divulging how deeply she felt for Knox would be off-putting.

"I dinnae believe Knox is ready to settle with a wife."

Liam's head tilted to the side as he studied her face. "Have ye made that presumption or has he stated it?"

Her first instinct was to run, the second was to scream loudly and stomp her feet. The situation was becoming absurd. How many were aware of a connection between herself and Knox? Had he said something to the men he considered friends?

Perhaps it would be best if she gave up the idea of marrying someone at the keep and instead found a husband among the men from the village.

Standing her ground, she gave Liam a direct look. "I ken it to be true."

He nodded. "I see."

As it was obvious the man had no intention of pursuing her if she had feelings for someone he considered a friend, Sencha began walking toward the door.

"It is best I return inside. My aunt and uncle will be retiring for the night and will be searching for me."

Rounding Liam, she hurried from where he stood, just as Knox walked out. He stopped and looked from her to Liam, who remained by the garden wall. Then frowning he turned to her.

When he started to say something, Sencha huffed and walked past him into the house. She'd not remain there at the keep but instead she'd go to the village with her aunt and uncle the next day.

SENCHA CARRIED A basket with items from the market as she headed back to her aunt and uncle's home. Entering the bakery next, she greeted the robust rosy-cheeked woman inside. The baker's wife seemed to be in a perpetual good mood and grinned widely at seeing Sencha.

"Two loaves today? I also have this one made with hearty oat grain." She rocked a round loaf of bread as if it were a bairn.

Once leaving the bakery, a man approached her. He looked to be perhaps thirty with a thick neck and muscular arms. She recognized him as the blacksmith, from the couple of times Gordon had sought him out.

"Yer the MacTavish lass aren't ye?" he said walking alongside. "I will help ye with the basket."

Sencha glanced at him. "I dinnae require help."

Undeterred he kept in step with her. "Perhaps I can take ye for a walk this eve?"

Although the man was rugged and nice-looking, she wasn't attracted to him. "I am nae interested," Sencha replied, then feeling bad for being so abrupt she added, "I appreciate yer kind offer."

"Are ye spoken for then?" The man persisted.

"I am..." Sencha stopped talking, her throat seizing as she couldn't formulate words. Her heart was spoken for, but in reality, she was not. In a panic, she turned to the man beside her. "What am I doing? He declared his feelings and I rebuffed him." To her horror, tears began spilling from her eyes. "What it must have taken for him to say such things. I am sure he has never said them before."

The blacksmith froze, unsure what to do as she blurted out words while crying. "I am nae sure what to tell ye, lass."

"I must make things right." Sencha shoved the basket at him and walked in a circle. "But how? I have made such a mess of things. I was judgmental, prideful, and unbending. It is I who is nae willing to make changes. The poor man was honest and open. And what did I do? I laughed." She held both hands over her mouth and stared up at the blacksmith.

"I laughed." Sencha threw her hands in the air. "I laughed until I cried." Her voice pitched.

Meeting the man's gaze she blew out a breath. "I must make things right. Should I not?"

The blacksmith's expression told her that he thought her to be mad. "I suppose."

"Thank ye." She grabbed the basket from him and attempted a smile, which she was sure looked more like a grimace. "Ye have been very helpful."

THE STEW SMELLED delicious, rich with herbs and tender chunks of venison, but Sencha could barely manage more than a couple of spoonfuls. Each time she tried, her stomach twisted in knots. She reached for a piece of oat loaf, tearing off a small portion and biting into it absentmindedly. The soft crunch of the bread seemed louder than it should have, echoing her unease. She set the remainder of the loaf beside her bowl, her appetite dwindling with every passing second.

"Ye may as well tell us what's eating at ye, lass," her aunt quipped, her sharp gaze dropping pointedly to the barely touched food in front of Sencha.

Glancing down, Sencha noticed she'd scattered crumbs and torn bits of bread all around her bowl, the evidence of her distraction. She shrugged, willing her voice to sound casual. "I am preoccupied, that is all," she replied lightly, grasping for a change of topic. "I do quite enjoy village life, though. Perhaps, once I marry, I'll live here."

Her aunt wasn't so easily deterred. With an expression both knowing and patient, she folded her arms. "Are ye sure it is nae someone, perhaps a handsome archer, who has yer mind elsewhere?"

Before Sencha could respond, her uncle Donald interjected, "Jane, let the girl keep her thoughts to herself." He spoke around a mouthful of stew, his tone gruff yet laced with warmth.

But her aunt wasn't one to give up so easily. "Do tell me,"

she pressed, her tone teasing. "Is it that handsome archer who's captured yer heart and mind? Knox, was it?"

Heat flared across Sencha's cheeks, but she fought to keep her expression neutral. Instead of replying, she busied herself with her spoon, stirring the stew as though she hadn't heard the question. Finally she followed her uncle's lead and took another bite. The savory broth warmed her throat, but it did little to ease her discomfort. She shook her head slightly, avoiding her aunt's piercing gaze.

When her aunt chuckled knowingly, the sound seemed to pierce right through Sencha's defenses. She swallowed and finally spoke, her voice low. "I have lost any opportunity with Knox," she admitted reluctantly. "I didnae believe him ready to settle."

Her aunt opened her mouth to reply, but this time, it was her uncle who spoke first. "Ah, lass," he said, leaning back in his chair with a satisfied sigh, his bowl nearly empty. "A man never thinks himself ready to settle—not until the right woman comes along."

His gaze flicked to his wife, a soft chuckle rumbling in his chest. "No man thinks himself prepared for it until it happens. It can be rather surprising?"

Her aunt Jane's expression softened as their eyes met, a quiet understanding passing between them. Sencha watched the exchange with a mixture of fondness and envy. She felt a pang in her chest, the weight of her earlier choices pressing down on her. Knox's declaration echoed in her mind and guilt pricked at her heart. She'd dismissed him too quickly and perhaps unfairly.

"I must go to the keep tomorrow," she said abruptly, setting her spoon down. Her voice came out steadier than she'd expected, though her thoughts swirled in turmoil.

"Oh?" her aunt inquired, arching a brow. "And what takes ye there?"

"To see Nala," Sencha replied, perhaps a bit too quickly. The name tumbled out as a convenient excuse, though it wasn't entirely untrue. She'd speak to Nala and perhaps get her advice as to what to do.

Her aunt and uncle exchanged amused looks, the kind that made Sencha's stomach churn anew. She could practically hear their unspoken thoughts, their unvoiced questions. Her aunt's lips twitched, as though she wanted to say more, but for once, she held her tongue.

Sencha pushed back her chair, rising from the table before her aunt could start teasing again. "Thank ye for the meal," she said quietly. Without waiting for a reply, she stepped away, the sound of their murmured laughter following her as she slipped into the next room.

CHAPTER FIFTEEN

T HE AIR WAS crisp with the sharp bite of oncoming winter, a constant reminder that colder days were swiftly approaching. Frost clung to the edges of the underbrush, and the breath of Knox's steed puffed out in soft white clouds as they rode through the narrowing forest path. Soon, the chill would drive most people indoors and only those with pressing matters would venture out into the biting cold.

Knox rode alongside Hendry, the hooves of their horses crunching through a thin layer of frost-dusted leaves. The day was unusually quiet. No patrols to lead. No drills to conduct. No guard posts to oversee. It was rare to have a day unencumbered by duties, but Knox wasn't entirely at ease. His mind was far too preoccupied for idle rest.

"Where exactly is this cottage?" Knox asked, breaking the silence as the pair moved deeper into the woods. The skeletal branches above cast shadows that danced over the ground, their jagged lines stretching and shifting with the afternoon light.

Hendry pointed toward the east, his gloved hand steady. "Not much farther now," he replied. "I'm checking on a widow. She was quite ill last time I visited, though she assured me her sister would come to care for her."

Knox nodded, casting a glance at his friend. Hendry had

always been one to look out for others, especially those who might otherwise be forgotten—an admirable quality, one Knox had long respected. It was good to be out riding together, as he hadn't wanted to linger at the keep. Sencha's cool rebuff still weighed heavily on his thoughts.

"And after this?" Knox asked, hoping to steer his mind elsewhere.

"We'll head to my parents' home," Hendry said with a faint grin. "Mother will be frying fish, as she does most afternoons when I visit. Ye'd be hard-pressed to find a better meal on the isle."

Knox's stomach growled in response, and he chuckled, patting his midsection. "I look forward to it. Yer mother's fish is unmatched—light, crisp, and perfectly seasoned. If I could trade guard duty for her cooking, I'd take it in a heartbeat."

Hendry smirked, his blue eyes glinting with mischief. "Perhaps she'll adopt ye, though I warn ye, she'd have ye splitting logs before the sun rose each morning."

The friendly banter eased the tension in Knox's chest, but it didn't erase it. Hendry must have noticed, for his smile dimmed, his gaze turning appraising.

"Ye've been acting different," Hendry said after a moment, his voice quiet yet probing. "Like someone who's lost his favorite possession. Forlorn, I'd call it."

Knox inhaled deeply, his gaze lifting to the towering trees that bordered the path. Their gnarled branches stretched toward the heavens, as if reaching for answers even they could not grasp. "Forlorn, am I?" he muttered, a dry note in his tone.

"Aye," Hendry replied, his eyes sharp with observation. "What bothers ye? Is it the lass? Sencha?"

Knox stiffened, his shoulders tensing. He considered denying it outright, but Hendry had known him since boyhood. His friend would see through any lie as easily as a hawk spotting prey. Reluctantly, Knox exhaled, his breath misting in the cool air.

"I am nae forlorn," he said slowly. "I have merely been considering what comes next in life. I suppose we all reach a point where decisions must be made."

Hendry laughed, shaking his head. "Knox, we are far too young to be at such a juncture. Is that nae when a man decides how he will live out his last days? We've years yet before that kind of thinking."

Knox smirked faintly but shook his head. "Nae, it is more than that. What I ponder is the time when a man chooses a path as in marriage, a new home, a change in profession…"

"Or getting a dog?" Hendry interjected, a teasing lilt in his voice.

Knox huffed a short laugh. "Aye, or getting a dog," he said, though his tone lacked conviction.

"And which juncture are ye at, then?" Hendry asked, tilting his head.

Knox hesitated, the weight of the unspoken truth pressing on him. He'd been toying with the idea of marriage, of building a life with Sencha, but her cold reaction to him had left those ideas in tatters. He wasn't ready to admit it aloud, not even to Hendry.

"Getting a dog," he finally replied, his voice clipped, hiding the truth behind a veil of humor.

Hendry raised a brow, clearly unconvinced, but he let the matter drop. "Well, a dog would suit ye," he said lightly.

"Though I suspect ye'll find a way to make even that decision more complicated than it needs to be."

Knox chuckled softly, but the sound carried no mirth. As they rode on, the tension in his chest remained, gnawing at him like an unwelcome shadow.

A SMALL BUT well-kept cottage came into view. A large black dog rounded from the back and watched them, its ears pinned back.

"Not a friendly sort," Hendry said slowly dismounting.

The dog lowered its head and studied Hendry, then sniffed the air, but didn't advance.

"Ailith!" Hendry called out. "It is Hendry!"

A few moments later a woman came from the back of the cottage and Knox's brows hitched at the sight of a comely woman who didn't look to be older than five and twenty.

The woman stopped at a short fence, her gaze moving from Hendry to Knox. "As ye can see, I am recovered. No need to trouble yerself coming by."

Hendry studied the woman for several beats. "I thought ye were to go to the village."

Once again the woman looked to Knox, and he recognized her. She was Brant's widow, one of the men who'd served as a Ross guard. What was Hendry thinking? The woman detested the guardsman, blaming him for her late husband's death.

"We should go," he said to Hendry. "She seems to be doing well."

The woman glared in his direction. "Knox Ross, I hear ye almost died saving a woman." Her words dripped with the insinuation that he'd not done the same for her husband.

"Ailith, ye look well." He turned his attention back to Hendry. "It seems Hendry's tending helped ye recover."

Despite her obvious dislike of him, Knox had to admit the woman was fetching. She was curvy with a generous bosom and a small waist that flared out to full hips. It was easy to see why Ailith caught Hendry's attention.

"Do ye require anything? I can bring ye something upon our return from near the village," Hendry asked, his tone even.

Expecting a terse reply, Knox tensed.

Surprisingly, the woman seemed to consider Hendry's question, then shook her head. "I have all I need. My sister came and brought plenty of food for myself and Teller."

"Very well," Hendry returned to his horse and mounted.

As they drove away, Knox looked over his shoulder, the woman remained by the gate, the dog at her side.

"It seems she has not forgotten nor lessened her dislike of us," Knox said. "Although I must admit, she seemed a bit receptive to ye."

Hendry shook his head. "Dinnae be deceived. I believe she would nae cry at my grave," he hesitated before continuing. "A woman like her should nae be living alone in such a desolate place. It is dangerous."

"I agree," Knox replied, considering that he'd hate it if Sencha lived at that cottage in the woods away from people. "She is bonny."

"Aye, she is. She is also quite contrary," Hendry said.

When Knox chuckled, he got a questioning look from the other man. "What is it?"

"Ye have a battle before ye if ye plan to pursue her. She considers ye her enemy."

"I dinnae have any such plans. If I pursue anyone, it will nae be someone who would have nae qualms stabbing me whilst I sleep." Hendry chuckled.

"What of ye, I would nae think ye would give up so easily in yer pursuit of the bonny Sencha." Of course Hendry had to turn the subject away from himself.

"The woman refuses to believe in me. What can I do?" Knox gave a one-shouldered shrug, despite the feeling like he'd been stabbed in the chest.

After a moment Hendry looked at him. "I can understand her hesitance. I am sure ye do as well. It may take work on yer part. But I have never known ye to act this way about a woman. Yer feelings must be strong."

Knox was silent as he thought. "It is nae a good feeling not to be believed in. Not to be trusted." All his life, he'd made sure to be the fighter others would wish to have at their back. He'd been a loyal and devoted member of Clan Ross and although admittedly roguish, not once had he forced or pushed a woman beyond where they wished to go. If anything, women pursued him. This was not exactly a good excuse for his actions, but at the same time he couldn't help that he adored the fairer sex.

Looking up to the sky, he wondered who Sencha would accept courtship from. The very idea made his stomach sour. And yet, he knew she would marry. How could she not? The woman was beautiful and alluring and like no other.

"Ye should try once again," Hendry said studying him.

Looking forward, Knox gave his friend a bland look. "I never took ye for a counselor."

CHAPTER SIXTEEN

A LEXANDER ENTERED THE great room and looked about the people gathered. Despite the fact it would be a busy day, with so many waiting for an audience the air in the room felt light. After so much chaos and danger, disputes between people was an easy task.

When a soft hand slipped into his, he didn't have to look to ken it was Nala. He turned to find his wife frowning up at him. "Ye left the bedchamber without speaking. Is all well?"

Not caring that there were others around, Alexander bent, wrapped the beauty in his arms and kissed her soundly.

There were murmurs and chuckles as he released the now blushing Nala, who looked around with round eyes. "Alex." Although she attempted to give him a stern reprimanding look letting him ken that type of behavior was not acceptable, the corners of her lips twitched.

"I apologize for leaving without talking to ye. I thought ye required rest and I didnae wish to disturb ye."

She leaned into his side as they made their way to the high board. There was no other place he ever wished his wife to be.

First meal was brought to them, and he ate without hesitation. Having made love and then talked until late into the night before another bout of love making had left him ravenous. He looked to Nala, who seemed to be just as hungry.

"Why would ye think anything was wrong? After the night we had, I expected ye to be sleeping in."

Although her complexion was a becoming shade, a result of a Caribbean mother and Scottish father, her cheeks darkened as she blushed. "What has gotten into ye. Ye need to not speak so loudly."

"I am a fulfilled husband. With a perfect wife," he teased, then whispered. "I love ye, Nala."

There was a commotion in the back of the great room as a man hurried in followed by two guardsmen. His personal guards moved closer to his back as the man neared.

The man was well-built, young, perhaps late twenties with a beard and thick arms. He slowed as he neared to assure the guards he meant no harm.

"Laird, danger comes to our lands. Ye must send warriors to the western shore."

Knowing his men regularly patrolled that shore, Alexander wasn't sure what the man stated was true. Although the western shore was exposed to the open sea, anyone planning some sort of attack would be confronted by two strong clans as a portion belonged to Clan Grant.

"Do I ken ye?" Alexander asked.

Alexander stood and rounded the table, placing himself between the man and his wife. Then he motioned for Cynden and Liam to come and the warriors came to stand beside him.

The man shook his head. "I have only arrived a pair of months ago, I am called Niven McConnell. I am nephew to Maira and Malcolm McConnell. They grow old and require help with the farm, so I came to help."

The McConnell's were indeed elderly and were checked on

every sennight by the men when patrolling. They were a kindly couple, who seemed to look forward to the visits.

"What did ye see?" Cynden asked.

"Two birlinns crowded with men came ashore late last night. I saw them when out for a walk. They were just south of where the farm is. They pulled the birlinns into the wooded area near there.

"My uncle said I should alert ye, so as soon as dawn broke, I rode here as fast as I could."

Alexander looked to Cynden. "Knox is meeting the patrol there this morning. Take twenty men and ride there immediately."

His cousin alone would be outmanned and could be taken or worse killed. He motioned to Liam to wait and returned his attention to Niven. "Were ye able to see their manner of dress, anything about them that gave ye any idea who they are?"

The man shook his head. "I went as near as I dared without them seeing me and hid behind trees to watch. They were quiet, so I could nae hear any accents. They wore warm clothing, fur cloaks, and thick boots."

There was the possibility they were travelers, who came ashore to rest. If not familiar with the area, they wouldn't ken where to send a messenger to alert the laird of their presence. After not so long ago being invaded by the McLeods, Alexander would take every precaution.

"Yer coming to alert me is much appreciated," he said to Niven. "Remain for a meal if ye wish."

Niven shook his head. "I must decline yer kind offer, but I wish to return as soon as possible and ensure my aunt and uncle are nae harmed."

"A pair of guardsmen will go with ye."

Once the men were dispatched and an obviously perturbed Liam remained, Alexander turned to the table. He gave his wife a reassuring look. He took a piece of bread, tore it open, and placed the other items on the plate into it, then turned to Liam. "To my study."

Once in the study, the guard and the leader overseeing the wall and gates joined them.

"Ensure all is well secured and every corner of the wall is manned. Wake the men who worked last night and make them aware of what happens, so they are mentally prepared tonight. Liam, the rest of the men who remain must be split, half inside the courtyard and the other outside the gates."

Liam nodded. "My men would prefer to go to the shore and defend our land."

"If it comes to it, ye can go later, right now I require men to remain here to ensure the safety of the keep."

The leader studied him. "Ye cannae go. Ye do understand that."

He'd already planned to ride with his personal guard needing to ken what occurred. "I cannae just remain here not knowing."

"A messenger will arrive as soon as the men get there and find out what happens," Liam rebutted. "Until then, ye must stay."

One of the most frustrating things of being laird was his limited battle engagement in defending his clan. He was a born warrior and staying behind the safety of walls went against his nature.

As much as he wanted to argue, he finally blew out a frustrated breath and looked to Liam. "Go see about the walls."

Once again Alex spoke to Liam. "Ensure the men posted around the outside are fully armed and remain alert. Instruct the ones inside to walk the perimeter constantly."

With that, he waited for the men to leave and then stalked back to the great room. There were the day-to-day duties to be seen to. After all, life didnae stop because of reports of people arriving on the shoreline.

THE RIDE TO the southern shore was long, but it was to be Knox's patrol area that day. His men would arrive soon after, so he took his time getting there. Having left Hendry's parent's home early that morning, he'd planned for a leisurely ride. Unfortunately, the time alone gave him the opportunity to think and revisit the last interaction he'd had with Sencha.

At the time when she'd repeated not believing he was ready to settle, Knox had not allowed her judgement to affect him. Part of the reason was his training as a warrior not to show emotion.

Truthfully, the main reason was that he'd been caught off guard. Not only by her reaction but by how deeply he cared for her. It was the first time he'd ever declared himself to a woman and had no idea how to prepare and what to expect.

One thing he knew for sure was that he'd not expected her to laugh or for her to be so certain in her lack of belief in him and his feelings. The more he pondered on it, the deeper her words cut. If only he'd waited, known that it was her mother marrying and not her, then he could have found out how she felt for him.

From the way she melted under his kisses and trembled at his caresses, it was clear Sencha wasn't immune to him. The woman had gone as far as to confess she had deep feelings for him. He'd felt triumphant in that moment.

If he continued to revisit the interactions between himself and Sencha again and again, he would go mad. If nothing else, he'd gained experience and would never dismiss heartbreak again. So many times he'd been annoyed when a member of his team had been disheartened over a woman.

So far into his thoughts, Knox looked around to gather his bearings. He was near the coast as the salty air reached his nostrils. The hairs on the back of his neck stood on end, a sense of foreboding taking over and he guided his horse away from the path and into a wooded area. Something was amiss.

Once in the safety of the trees, Knox dismounted and tethered his horse. Keeping low to the ground, he made his way on foot. Whenever he peered around trees and bushes, there wasn't anyone in sight. Yet the feeling of being watched kept him moving forward.

He stopped and leaned behind a tree hoping he hid in the right direction. Slowing his breath, he listened for any sounds that didn't belong.

The birds were silent, a good indicator that someone was about. Of course it could be it was him that had quieted the feathered creatures.

Just as he was about to give up and return to the horse, there was a sound of more than one person nearby. Whoever they were they spoke in low tones, as if not wishing to be overheard.

Most hunters would speak softly, so it could be there wasn't anything to be worried about. And yet, these were the laird's lands, and no one was permitted to hunt unless first seeking permission. Since this was his area to patrol, he would have been informed of the grant.

Crouching low, he peered around the tree. In a small clearing, a group of men, perhaps six had gathered. None of them were familiar to him.

Just past them, two bìrlinns had been dragged into the woods, so they would not be visible from the shoreline or from the road.

Knox looked over his shoulder then to the ground to ensure he would not step on anything and moved backward. If the men were not friendly, it would not do to be caught alone. By the fact he had a sword strapped to his back, it would be obvious he was a warrior.

When a safe distance away, he straightened and hurried back to his horse, then stopped in his tracks. Two men stood by his horse looking straight at him.

Four other men came out from both sides and approached but kept a safe distance.

"Who are ye?" Knox asked. "These are Ross lands, ye must make yerselves known to my laird."

The men remained silent and exchanged looks.

When his horse bobbed his head and neighed, getting everyone's attention, Knox pulled his sword from its sheath. "Answer me," he called out whilst turning side to side. He wouldn't last long against so many. His only hope was that his team of six men would arrive in time.

"Let me guess," one of the men said approaching. The

others looked on, so it seemed the man was possibly their leader. "Ye are a guard to this Laird Ross?"

The man's accent was unfamiliar, perhaps from another isle or they could be a gang of rogue criminals who'd come together.

Keeping his eyes moving, he met the man's gaze. "I am."

"Unfortunately for ye, it is best nae to leave anyone who has seen us." The man looked back at Knox's horse. "How to make it seem as if ye met an unfortunate end that had nothing to do with another person?"

One of the others chuckled. "Some men hang themselves." He eyed the horse. "Stand on the horse, throw a rope, and complete the deed."

Thankfully Knox didn't have a rope and from a quick scan he gathered neither did any of the idiots surrounding him.

The man motioned to everyone with both hands. "I need a better idea."

"Fell off the horse and broke his neck."

"Hit his head on a rock."

"Trampled by the horse."

The ideas, although creative would be hard to pull off, because Knox had no intention of being taken without a fight.

"What about the dead bodies they find lying about?" he countered.

The spokesman nodded toward him as if in approval. "There is that."

Despite the strange conversation, Knox was not fooled for one moment. These men were dangerous, they fled from somewhere and didn't want to be found out.

One of the men closest to him, a younger one, took a step

back and narrowed his eyes. "I say we cut him through and throw him into the water."

"He will wash up," another countered. "We should kill him and go."

"Not until we find food. We must get something to eat," the leader countered. He turned to Knox. "Where is the nearest house?"

Knox gave him an incredulous look. "Should I slaughter a pig and roast it for ye?" If he was about to die, he would not show any fear. What bothered him was that once they killed him, they would probably find the nearby farm and kill the defenseless people who lived there. The elderly couple, who lived at the nearest farm wouldn't have a chance.

"It is best ye leave. I am sure word of yer arrival will have reached the laird by now." At least it was what Knox hoped, although he doubted it. They didn't patrol this coastline during the night.

The leader of the group motioned to Knox. "Best to kill him and bury the body. He will nae be found." He then pointed to one of the men standing by the horse. "Take the steed and find the nearest house. Return quickly so we can be on our way."

Then he looked to those flanking Knox. "What are ye waiting for? Kill him."

As one man mounted and rode away, Knox's stomach sank. He would reach the farm before anyone could beat him there to stop him.

Hoping to defend himself for as long as possible, Knox turned from side to side watching the men surrounding him. His sword out, he pulled a dagger from his belt and palmed it in his left hand. His aim with the dagger was reliable, so he turned to the left and threw it. The dagger sunk into the younger man's chest. Caught by surprise, he stumbled backward dropping the blade he held.

Not waiting to see what happened, Knox palmed a second dagger. He only had three, which was unfortunate.

As the duo on his right advanced, he flung a second dagger at the one in front; unfortunately, he missed the chest and it sunk into the man's shoulder. Still it was a good hit as it was the man's sword arm. The man yelled but continued advancing. Thankfully, the pain must have kept him from thinking clearly because when he pulled the dagger free. Blood spurted from the wound and for a moment the man hesitated pressing his hand over the wound. He swayed side to side before passing out.

As the man on his left advanced, he swung his sword effectively blocking him and then he quickly turned to the right to defend against another. He wouldn't last long, but at least he'd wound them enough to make it easier for his men.

"Kill him!" the idiot who continued to stand watching called out, and motioned for the other one standing next to him to join in.

Knox jumped backward to avoid being hit, causing the two men on his sides to turn to avoid striking each other. Reaching for the third dagger as he tried his best to block the three advancing men, he knew it would be best to aim for the leader, but the man was a distance away. Instead he opted for the one who had been to his left.

Before he could throw the dagger, the trio advanced all at once, swords held high. With no other option, Knox turned and took off running.

He ran toward the road he'd been on, hoping to be out in the open where he could be seen. Thankfully, he was used to physical exertion and was able to put a bit of distance between himself and his pursuers.

Upon reaching the road, he turned and waited for the three to get closer, then he threw the dagger at the one in front. He missed.

The man bent and picked up the dagger, then threw it in his direction. Knox managed to avoid it, but just barely. He was growing tired.

Once again, he ran. His sword in hand. The men were talking to one another, and he expected they were formulating a plan.

When something hard hit him in the back, Knox realized they'd thrown a rock. He had to admit it was a good plan, but not a deadly one. So he began running in an unpredictable pattern, hoping to keep from being hit.

One of the men was catching up to him. If he were to guess, it was the one who'd not been fighting.

Taking a deep breath, he glanced over his shoulder and then when the man was close enough to strike, Knox came to a dead stop, turned with his sword straight out, and cut the man across his midsection.

The man let out a loud yowl, but not seeming to realize the extent of his injuries, he lifted his weapon and swung. Knox blocked the strike and countered by cutting into the injured man's side. The strike must have brought awareness, because the man looked to his gaping stomach and dropped to his knees. Grasping his midsection, he began to moan whilst kicking his legs out in pain.

The other two circled Knox, their eyes moving from him to the man who thrashed on the ground dying.

"I am nae easy prey," Knox called out. "Take yer chances if ye must."

One of them let out a loud growl and advanced, while the other man came up behind him. It was then shouts sounded nearby. Knox didn't have to look to ken Ross warriors had arrived.

The eyes of his attackers widened, and they turned and raced back into the trees. No doubt to alert the others of what came.

It wasn't just his team, but two. There were at least twenty men, more than enough to rid their lands of the opponents.

Cynden Ross brought his horse to a stop and jumped down. The laird's youngest brother neared and looked him over. "Ye should sit." He took Knox by the arm. "Now."

"I dinnae need to sit."

The warrior gave him a droll look. "Believe me, ye do."

Knox held his arms out and turned in a circle. "I am perfectly well."

"Ye should inform yer left arm of that."

It was then he looked to his left bicep and noted the wound. One of the idiots had cut his arm open.

"That must be why I missed," he said and swayed. "Someone must go to the McConnell's. One of them took my horse and headed there to find food. He will probably kill them. There are three of them left in the woods and seven more camped just past the bend." He pointed and hissed in pain when he tried to lift his injured arm.

Annoyed that he couldn't go with the men to fight the intruders, Knox allowed Cynden to help him to sit. A wagon appeared that had been dispatched to tend to any injured and moments later Knox was in the back of it. The healer wasted no time washing out the wound and stitching it closed.

Since he'd barely eaten that morning and had downed an entire wineskin whilst being sewn up, Knox was unable to fight the sleep that claimed him.

When he opened his eyes, the sun was still up, and he was still in the back of the wagon. He sat up grimacing, at the pain brought by the movement.

The healer looked to him. "Ye had another cut on yer upper back. I stitched it up as well."

"Thank ye," Knox said and looked around. "How long did I sleep? Have the warriors nae returned?"

Hendry's face loomed over him. "A messenger was sent to Alexander. We think all of them have been dealt with swiftly."

"What about the McConnells?" he asked, fighting the urge to close his eyes.

"They were found well, their nephew is there. He is who alerted us to the intruders. We have nae found the man who took yer horse. We hope yer horse will return to the keep on its own if left unattended."

Knox gritted his teeth. "I must find my steed." He slid to the end of the wagon. "Hendry, get me a horse."

"I dinnae think it wise for ye to ride at the moment," the healer said in a patient voice. "There were herbs in the wine. I would be surprised if ye can stand."

Not willing to listen, Knox placed both feet on the ground and stood. It lasted only a moment before he stumbled sideways. Thankfully Hendry caught him or else he would have landed on the ground.

Hendry walked him back to the wagon and helped him to sit. "We will find both the man and yer steed. Tomorrow is soon enough for ye to join in the search. Already our warriors, led by Liam, are on the hunt. If anyone can find him, it is he."

CHAPTER SEVENTEEN

INSTEAD OF GOING to the keep, Sencha had been taken home by her uncle, who insisted she should discuss things with her mother before proceeding.

Sencha had no such plans and kept insisting she wanted to go visit Nala.

For the past several days that she'd been home, it had been different. Despite the fact her mother was practically floating on air, which made Sencha happy, she felt as if she were at someone else's home.

Strange how Gordon had lived there for as long as Sencha could remember, sleeping in a small room on the first floor, and yet it felt so very different now.

In deference to her deceased father, her mother informed Sencha she was not comfortable for Gordon and her to use that same room. So they'd exchanged bedchambers with Sencha, and she now slept in what used to be her mother's room.

Although the rooms were almost the same size, the view out of the window faced the road and she wasn't used to the sun rising into the room in the morning. She wondered if perhaps the change in the way she felt about her home had more to do with her feelings toward Knox. The insistent constant reminder that she'd rebuffed his proposal.

There were so many other options she could have chosen. She could have asked that they court and see how he felt over time. Now she wasn't sure how to feel, what to think.

The practical thing to do was to go to the keep and speak to him.

Her mother looked to Gordon. "Can ye take her?"

"I can ask another farmhand to take me. No need to put yerself out," Sencha replied, not wishing to have to travel with Gordon and make small talk.

He gave her a knowing smile. "I think it would be a good idea for me to take ye. I want to visit with the stable master and see how the horses they purchased are faring."

"Horses?" Sencha asked, not aware the laird's stable had bought horses.

"Aye," Gordon said. "One of the archers lost his horse and he sent the stable master to purchase one of ours." The man puffed out his chest with pride. "I suppose he must have seen them and admired them when we went to the keep last."

"They are of good stock," her mother added. "Athol did well in choosing them."

Since there was no putting off Gordon, Sencha pushed back from the table. "Very well. I will pack an overnight satchel and remain a day or two. I will ask that someone from there bring me back."

ADMITTEDLY, THE RIDE to the keep was pleasant enough. Sencha and Gordon had always had an easy rapport, and their conversations were the same as before. Sencha wasn't sure why she'd thought things would be different. In a way, it was simpler now that she didn't have to pretend to nae know how he felt about her mother whenever they were alone.

Upon arriving at the keep, she was helped from the wagon by a guard who insisted on carrying her overnight satchel.

Learning that Nala was in the sitting room, Sencha hurried past the great room, her skirts brushing the stone floors as she went. The murmur of voices and the distant clatter of the servants at work faded as she turned down the quieter corridor. She found her friend seated by a tall window, the late afternoon light casting soft shadows across the room. Nala's expression was distant, her gaze fixed on something far beyond the glass.

As soon as she noticed Sencha, Nala rose swiftly, her lips curving into a small but warm smile. "I am so happy ye're here," she said, crossing the room to embrace her. Her voice carried a weariness that her smile couldn't quite conceal. "It has been a trying pair of days."

"What has happened?" Sencha asked, her brows knitting with concern.

Before Nala could reply, a servant entered the room carrying a tray. Nala turned to her with a nod of gratitude. "Perfect timing, Milly. This is much needed."

She took the tray herself, dismissing the servant, and gestured for Sencha to sit. "Come," Nala urged, motioning to a cushioned chair near the low table where the tray was placed. "Sit, please, so we can talk. Alexander's mother and Ainslie have gone to visit Munro and Lila for a pair of days, and I find myself without company."

Sencha's lips twitched in amusement. "I doubt that's entirely true," she said, settling into the chair. "There are plenty of women in the keep who would be glad to spend time with ye."

Nala sighed, lifting the small kettle from the tray. "Perhaps, but it's nae the same. Being the laird's wife comes with its own set of restrictions. It can feel isolating at times." She poured steaming water over the herbs she'd already prepared in the cups, and a fragrant, earthy aroma filled the room.

"This is a tea Belhar brought me during his last visit," Nala said, a flicker of fondness lighting her face. "He brought enough to last me until they return again."

Sencha accepted the cup with a nod of thanks, inhaling the exotic scent. It reminded her of late autumn evenings, when the hearth fires burned low, and warmth was found in small comforts. "I'd forgotten Athol and Belhar usually return in the winter," she said thoughtfully. "Hopefully they will remain through the cold season until the sea calms in the spring."

Nala gave a small nod, her smile fading slightly. "Athol will be surprised to learn yer mother has married."

"I imagine so," Sencha agreed, watching her friend closely. Something in Nala's manner—the restless way her fingers smoothed over her gown, the slight crease in her brow suggested there was more troubling her than she let on. Sencha had known Nala all her life and could read her easily.

"There has been trouble." Sencha ventured gently, her tone inviting honesty.

Nala hesitated, her gaze drifting to the window again. For a moment it seemed she might deny it, but then she sighed deeply. "Aye," she admitted. "There were intruders on the western shore two nights past. Our warriors dealt with them."

Her words were calm, but her fingers tightened around her cup. Sencha's eyes narrowed. "There's more to it than that."

Nala's hesitation was answer enough. She set her cup down and leaned forward slightly, as though bracing herself. "One of them got away," she confessed, her voice barely above a whisper. "He may not be a threat, but there is no way of knowing. He took a horse."

Sencha took a slow sip of the tea. Its warmth soothing her throat, even as unease prickled at her. She considered her friend's words, weighing their implications. "It seems that other than the man who escaped, the situation is under control," she said carefully. "But ye seem bothered."

Nala's lips lifted into a faint, bittersweet smile. "Melancholy," she murmured. "Why must there always be strife and danger? It feels as though one thing follows another in a never-ending cycle. Is peace truly so fleeting?"

Sencha reached out, her hand brushing Nala's in a gesture of reassurance. "We endure, as we always do," she said softly. Then, after a pause, she added, "What of Knox? Is he here?"

At the mention of Knox's name, Nala's gaze flickered to her, then back to the window. "I dinnae ken his duties," she replied after a moment. "He is usually at the last meal of the day."

"I will wait and speak to him then," Sencha said decisively, setting her cup down.

Nala reached across the table, placing a hand firmly over Sencha's. Her touch was gentle, but her words carried a quiet urgency. "Perhaps it is best that ye dinnae."

Sencha blinked, startled by the unexpected suggestion. She searched her friend's face, trying to decipher the meaning behind the words. "Why?" she asked, her voice laced with confusion.

But Nala only withdrew her hand, her expression unreadable. "Just trust me on this," she said quietly, turning her gaze once more to the view outside.

JUST THEN A pair of women entered, and Sencha recognized them. Both were married to guardsmen and often came to the keep for meals if their husbands were on gate duty.

In an instant, Nala transformed into the laird's wife, a welcoming expression as she showed the women to other chairs in the room. She then turned to a servant who'd followed behind. "Bring more water and cups."

Apparently the women were expected by the way they immediately delved into a discussion of upcoming preparations for winter. One of Nala's duties was to take baskets of food and warm blankets to the elderly and infirm in the surrounding lands before winter set in. Before her, Alexander's mother had done the duty. It was expected.

Along with the baskets of food and warm blankets, guardsmen would accompany the women and ensure there was enough chopped wood to keep the people warm through the winter.

As the discussion continued, Sencha's mind kept returning to what Nala had stated. Curiosity getting the better of her, she excused herself and left the room.

There were only a few people meandering in the great room, more than likely those who hoped to speak to the laird.

Continuing on into the corridor leading to the kitchens, she saw only a pair of maids hurrying past with folded linens.

Sounds of pots clashing and voices came from the kitchen, and she continued down the corridor until arriving at the wide doorway. Inside the cook called out instructions as she walked about the room with a large spoon in her hand sniffing, sampling, and stirring.

The woman glanced over to Sencha, then turned away and continued her duties.

What exactly she would say to Knox, Sencha wasn't sure. Despite the many scenarios in her head, she wouldn't ken until facing him. Her mind awhirl, she absently walked outside and turned toward the practice field.

A few men spared, while others stood by watching. There were no archers in sight. One by one, she studied the men, but none were Knox. It would be best to wait until last meal, since according to Nala, he was usually present.

Just then she noticed a lone man standing near the stables. He faced away from her as he watched another man inside the corral with the horses. The man had what looked to be a sling across his wide back. It was then she realized who it was.

It was Knox.

Immediately her heart began to pound. He'd been injured, his left arm apparently as he lifted the right one and raked his hair back.

Making her way across the courtyard, Sencha couldn't look away. Had he always been so tall and well-built? Of course he had. It was just that she saw him through different eyes now. Saw him as the man she was in love with.

As she neared, he turned and upon seeing her, his eyes widened for a second before returning his attention to the horse.

It was Gordon who was in the corral, the older man gave her a warm look. "This was our largest horse. He is of good stock and does nae scare easily," Gordon told Knox, who looked on with lowered brows.

"Did ye forget something, lass?" Gordon asked her.

Sencha shook her head. "Dinnae tarry. Ye should get home before it becomes dark, else Mother will worry."

Gordon looked up to the sky, as if for confirmation. "Right ye are. I should head back." He looked at Knox. "Once ye are able ride the horse. We have others if ye wish for a different one."

"I am sure this one will suit me just fine," Knox replied.

"One does nae ken until ye mount," Gordon remarked as he removed the rope from around the horse's face and walked from the corral.

"Were ye injured by the men who came from ashore?" she asked Knox, who gave a single nod.

Before she could say anything else, Gordon exited the stables and talked to Knox once again about the horse. Then patting her shoulder and assuring her he'd be home before dark, he climbed onto the wagon's bench and drove away.

From his stiff posture and the way he kept his eyes to the horse, Knox was not exactly welcoming conversation.

"I need to speak with ye," Sencha began, her voice soft but insistent. "I need to explain."

"Not now, Sencha." His tone cut through the air, sharp with anger—or was it pain? Maybe both.

She faltered, uncertain. "I understand—"

"Do ye?" Knox turned to her, his eyes hard, his lips a grim line. "I doubt that."

Her heart clenched. It struck her then that he was the warrior who'd lost his horse. He'd been injured, his pride battered, and now he was staring at her as if she was part of the wreckage. The realization stole her breath.

"I'm sorry," she whispered, daring to reach for him. But as her hand hovered near his arm, he leaned away, the rejection as sharp as a blade.

Sencha's hand fell to her side, her chest tight with unspoken words. Every part of her wanted to stay, to comfort him, to tell him she'd stand by him no matter what. But his walls were unyielding. She could see it in his stance, hear it in the icy distance of his voice.

She turned and walked away, her heart fracturing with every step. She wanted so desperately to be his solace, to give him the reassurance he needed. But how could she when, in his eyes, she was part of a bad time? Injured, humiliated, and grieving his horse, he had no place for her. Not now.

CHAPTER EIGHTEEN

T HERE WAS THE pounding of hooves and sounds of voices as a group of guardsmen returned after a long day of patrolling. Six men and six horses, and the grim set to the men's faces meant they'd not found the man nor Knox's horse.

With practiced graceful movements, Hendry dismounted, handed the horse's reins to another guard, and strode toward the well where Knox stood. The warrior's fur-lined cloak made him bulkier and more menacing. Pulling water from the well, Hendry used the cup on a sting next to it and scooped water to drink. "How is yer arm?"

"Not as sore. My men have nae returned as yet. I will mount tomorrow."

"Wait until the day after," Hendry replied and turned to the house. "It was tiring. Nothing much to see."

Knox knew full well how taxing it was to be out as the days became frigid and one had to fight to keep warm.

They walked toward the house together so that Hendry could give his report to Alexander. Knox let out a breath. "Sencha is here."

With a soft grunt, Hendry shook his head. "She is close to Nala and will always visit."

He'd told Hendry about his declaration and the rejection. Although not one to normally share, it was what happened when one was injured and drank too much ale. Surprisingly, it had made him feel better to share.

"She asked to speak to me," Knox said, unsure why his mouth kept on. "I sent her away."

Hendry stopped and turned to him. "It may be best that ye hear what it is she has to say."

"What good would it do?"

The other guards caught up with them after leaving their steeds at the stable to be fed and brushed by the group of lads that worked there. The group went into the main house anxious for food and drink.

INSTEAD OF JOINING the others for last meal, Knox had retreated to his bedchamber, requesting food be brought to him. His chest felt heavy with frustration and weariness, the kind that settled deep in his bones. The loss of his horse gnawed at him, a dull ache that refused to relent. Gaisgeil wasn't just a horse; he was a loyal companion. An extension of himself. For twelve long years, they had braved countless battles and patrolled endless terrain.

The only hope now lay in Gaisgeil's intelligence and instincts. The horse was clever, and Knox clung to the fragile hope that the thief who'd taken him would be careless, failing to tether him properly, allowing the animal to break free and find his way back.

Gaisgeil had earned his name, meaning *brave* in their first year together. The horse had an uncanny ability to sense danger before Knox ever saw it coming. It was Gaisgeil's quick reactions that had saved his life on more than one occasion, whether in the chaos of battle or during the quiet, tense moments of an ambush. Losing him felt like losing a part of himself, a steady presence that had never wavered, no matter the storm.

Knox pushed the plates away, the half-eaten food now tasteless and forgotten. Rising abruptly, he strode to the window and threw the shutters open with a sharp motion. Cool air rushed in, carrying the faint, woodsy scent of the evening. He leaned against the sill, his shoulders tense, his eyes scanning the horizon.

For hours he stood there, his gaze unwavering as the sun dipped lower. The sky turned a fiery orange, bathing the world in a golden hue that softened the harsh lines of the land. The hills and trees cast long shadows over the valleys, and Knox's eyes searched for any sign of movement. A lone figure. The unmistakable silhouette of a horse.

But there was nothing. The fields stretched empty, and the stillness felt like a cruel joke. Knox blinked away the wetness gathering in his eyes, clenching his jaw to steady himself. He wasn't one to fall apart—not ever—but Gaisgeil was more than just a horse. He was a comrade. A piece of his soul.

A soft knock at the door broke the silence, and Knox exhaled sharply. No doubt a servant had come to collect the dishes. "Enter," he called out without turning, his voice rough from hours of silence.

"Knox."

The sound of her voice made his spine stiffen. It wasn't the servant, but Sencha. Her voice, wrapped around him like a balm to his frayed nerves, though he wished it didn't. Her presence was the last thing he needed. His hold on his emotions was tenuous at best which meant her presence forced him to rein in the storm swirling within, to keep control when control was the very thing slipping through his grasp.

"Why are ye here, Sencha?" he asked, his tone colder than he intended. He didn't turn. Couldn't. "Ye should nae be in my bedchamber."

The silence stretched, but he sensed her moving closer, her presence a faint warmth in the room. When he finally turned, his breath caught. Sencha stood near the center of the chamber, her hands clasped tightly before her chest. Her delicate features were etched with worry, her eyes shimmering with unshed tears. Even in her sadness, she was breathtaking—a timeless beauty with creamy skin and a softness that seemed to make everything warmer.

"Knox," she said, her voice trembling slightly. "if I am the reason ye remain here and didnae attend last meal, then I will return home immediately."

Her words struck him like a blow, and for a moment, he could only stare at her. What could he say? No matter his feelings, Sencha would always come to the keep. She was like a sister to Nala, and her presence would always be a constant.

"Once I say what I have to say, I will leave ye be," she continued, taking a tentative step closer. Her gaze never wavered, pinning his. "First, I want to tell ye how horrible I feel about the way I reacted when ye told me yer feelings."

Knox opened his mouth to reply, but her words came in a rush as though she needed to get them out before he could stop her.

"Understand me when I say this," she said, her voice breaking slightly. "At that time, so much was happening, and it was so unexpected. I was caught off guard, Knox. I didnae mean to hurt ye."

Her honesty pierced through him. He could see the anguish in her eyes, the way her shoulders tightened as though bracing for his response. And for the first time in days, he didn't feel anger or frustration, just a hollow ache, a quiet longing he couldn't suppress.

Unable to maintain eye contact lest he react as he wished and take her into his arms and lose himself in her. Instead, he turned back to the window.

"Ye dinnae have to explain anything."

Keeping his attention on the darkening view, all he wanted was for Sencha to stop the reminder of the humiliating moment. Unfortunately, he would have to hear her out. Listen to what she needed to get off her chest and then she'd leave.

"I am wrong to judge ye as to whether ye are ready to settle down with a wife. Ye are well enough aware of yer own feelings else ye would have never said what ye did. Apparently, I need a knock on the head to nae have appreciated yer words fully." She let out a shaky breath.

Letting out a long breath, Knox remained silent.

"Ye dinnae deserve it, how I reacted. I care for ye deeply Knox. I love ye, truly. I can only say fear made me react so flippantly about what ye declared."

"I understand. Fear is what brought me to speak out and say things I should have kept to myself until a better time."

Her hand pressed onto his shoulder, and he closed his eyes.

"I am so very sorry to have caused ye grief. I must ask that ye forgive me."

Knox turned to her, searching her eyes as though he could find the answer to everything in the depths of her gaze. His voice softened, a tender edge in every word. "There's naught to forgive, lass. Some of what ye said was true. I was uncertain, aye. But the one thing I knew, the one truth I could nae deny, was that I could nae bear to lose ye to another."

Her lips trembled into the faintest of smiles but doubt still lingered in her eyes. "Ye are a good man, Knox Ross."

Before she could say another word, he closed the space between them, capturing her mouth with his. It wasn't a kiss born of haste but one born of need. Pure need. The need to hold her. To claim her.

The taste of her, the warmth of her body yielding to his, sent a shiver through him. When she responded, tentative at first, her touch careful on his injured arm, it only fueled the fire in him.

The pain faded into irrelevance as he slid his uninjured arm around her waist, drawing her closer. The world seemed to fall away, leaving only this moment. Her in his arms. Her kiss igniting a sense of completeness he'd never known. It wasn't just passion that stirred within him but the profound feeling of finding his other half. She was the missing piece, the one who made him whole.

When the kiss ended, he rested his forehead against hers, his breath mingling with hers, his voice raw with emotion. "I love ye, Sencha. What I feel for ye—I've never felt anything like it before."

Her arms circled his waist, and she leaned into him, her voice a whisper yet strong with conviction. "I love ye too, Knox. With all my heart, my soul, with every piece of me."

"Will ye be my wife then?" He couldn't live another day without claiming her, without knowing she would be in his life for the rest of their days.

For a scant moment, Knox's gut tightened. Had he made the same mistake again? Caught her with an unexpected request at the wrong moment?

"Aye, I will. I wish for nothing more than to be yer wife," Sencha exclaimed, raising to her toes and kissing him on the lips. "I will be yer wife, Knox."

Pure joy surged through him. Overwhelming him to the point Knox thought his heart would burst. Tears swelled in his eyes, and he didn't bother to hide them. Sencha had a right to ken how deeply his feeling went.

The kiss that came next was laced with undeniable passion, their tongues mingling, hands touching, soft moans filling the space.

"I need more," Sencha uttered, as his mouth traveled down the side of her delectable neck. "I need."

Knox licked a trail to her ear. "I will give ye everything, once ye are my wife. Ye will never need for my touch."

Clasping his tunic she pressed against him, and he wanted to curse the sling. He continued to press kisses down the side of her neck, whilst untying the sling. The stitches would pull a bit, but it was worth it to have her flush against him.

"Oh, Knox." Her words were breathless as he'd trailed his lips to the top of her breasts where he continued to tease.

Whether it was her or him, they made their way to the edge of the bed.

WITHOUT SPEAKING, BOTH knew what the next step would be.

There was no stopping their trek toward becoming one both in body and mind. Sencha never ceased to amaze him as she began to help him lift his tunic up and over his head, taking care not to move his left arm more than needed. It took a bit of doing, but their clothing was done away with and both stood before each other, their gazes traveling over what they'd not seen before.

Unabashed, Sencha studied him from his head down to his feet. When her eyes hesitated at his thick erection her face reddened but she kept her gaze steady as she continued her perusal.

When it came to her, there was so much to take in. So many places he planned to spend months and years exploring. Her breasts were not large but would fill his hand. The slope of her waist that flowed gently to her hips begged to be caressed. Under her soft stomach, a small thatch of red enticed one to what lay beneath. Her legs were slender, perfect for throwing over his shoulders as he explored the very essence of her.

Unable to wait, he held out his hand and she took it. They moved closer to the bed, then he lay on his injured side and beckoned her to join him.

When Sencha lowered, he pulled her closer, immediately taking her mouth with his as he slid his right hand from her neck to her upper back. As bold as the lass was, he knew she had never been with a man and didn't wish to rush.

"At any moment, if ye wish to stop just say it. It is natural to be nervous or scared even. We have the rest of our days to be together."

She gave him a grateful look and nodded.

As he trailed his mouth, licking and nipping the creamy

skin as he went from her mouth down her neck until taking the tip of her breast and suckling gently.

Sencha gasped, her hands moving up and down his back, fingers digging into him as if wanting him to be closer.

Cupping her bottom, he pulled her against the hardness between his legs. Her moans filled his ears, the sounds so enticing it was like a beautiful song.

Rolling Sencha onto her back, he continued to kiss her breasts knowing he'd never grow tired of them, realizing he discovered true lovemaking for the first time.

His hand shook as he trailed it up the inside of her leg to her inner thigh, loving the way she quaked with passion and need.

"Knox," she gasped breathlessly when he pushed her legs apart and lowered until his mouth could take her in. First he flicked his tongue between her nether lips, then delved in, sliding his tongue into the moistness between.

Sencha lifted and lowered her hips as he continued licking, using his mouth to pleasure her. With a soft cry, she shuddered, legs shaking as she found her first release. He'd never heard a more beautiful sound.

He moved up to see that her eyes were closed, mouth agape as she gasped for air. "Can I take ye?" he asked his own voice breathless.

"Please. Please."

Still unsure of her ability to think clearly, he hesitated. Once he took her maidenhead, she would never be the same. And she would be fully his.

"Sencha," he said waiting for her eyes to open. They green gaze was unfocused, as she reveled in the aftereffects of having shattered.

"Are ye sure?"

She focused on him, her expression still soft. "I have never been surer of anything. I wish to be yers completely."

Reaching between her legs, he slid the pad of his middle finger over the nib in between the folds over and over until she began to climb again, her breathing in soft puffs.

Then taking himself in hand, he guided himself to her core. He was not a small man and feared hurting her. Proceeding carefully until nudging her entrance, he moved with deliberate slowness, allowing her to stretch and accommodate him.

Sencha's hands clung to his sides as he moved, her body still and tense.

"Relax. Breathe," he coached, lowering to take her mouth. He kissed her, somehow managing not to move from the precarious position his lower half was in until she responded. When he felt her tension ease he thrust into her.

Swallowing her cry, he held her in place, waiting for her to stop trembling. Sencha remained tense, undoubtedly fearing his movements would bring more pain. Thankfully she was wet, her sex receptive, so he began moving slowly, sliding out just a bit before moving back in.

It took several times before she relaxed and began to move into what became their rhythm of lovemaking.

She was so tight, so perfect, that Knox could not stop from peaking, his release making his entire body quake.

Breathless and spent, he managed to roll off Sencha and to her side. The slight pain on his left arm was worth it when compared to the fulfillment like he had never known. The sense that he'd found his perfect match in every way.

Sencha snuggled against him and sighed. "I cannae wait to be with ye every night."

"Neither can I," he replied, pressing a kiss to her brow. "Ye are perfect."

IT WAS MUCH too early when Sencha woke up the next morning. She stretched, a smile across her face as every movement brought a bit of discomfort. The thought of what brought it on, made her cheeks warm.

Allowing a bit of doubt for just a moment, she considered that it was possible Knox would wake and change his mind. Yes, it was possible and yet her heart knew he would not. They were deeply in love. His eyes, his body, every part of him was hers.

Slipping from the bed she hurried to the hearth and placed kindling into it then started the fire. She returned to the bed to wait for the room to warm, as she'd used plenty of wood, soon she was able to get out of bed to prepare for the day.

After washing with warmed water, she draped a shift then a long-sleeved pale blue blouse, followed by stockings and a heavy dark brown skirt. Finally, she topped the blouse with a vest matching the skirt.

A smile crept up as she finished dressing and then went to the window and pushed one of the shutters open allowing light from the cloudy day into the room. Then going to a chair, she began brushing the tangles from her hair. In her haste to go to bed, she'd not bothered to braid it.

Brushing her long hair, she wrapped it into a low bun and pinned it in place.

Allowing herself a few moments to gather her thoughts, Sencha peered out the window to a view of a bit shoreline on her left and still green lush hills to the right. The salty air filled her lungs. There was so much she didnae ken about Knox. Where his lands were? Would he wish for her to live in a house there or here at the keep? Admittedly, she wouldn't mind remaining at the keep and close to Nala. At the same time, having a home of her own was something she'd always wished for.

Then there was the matter of his roguish ways. She'd have to ask him how much of it was true. If there were other women in his life, he would have to put a stop to it immediately. One thing was for sure, she had no qualms about ending things if he refused.

A shepherd walked from where she supposed his home was to a group of sheep. The animals weren't bothered, allowing him near as he looked over them. She kept watch as the man moved from group to group obviously caring for his herd.

A knock sounded at her door. Strange that a chambermaid would come so early. Opening the door her breath left at seeing it was Knox standing there. He'd donned a clean tunic, and his hair was damp as if recently washed.

When his gaze roamed over her, it was as if he touched her, and Sencha held her breath until she was forced to release it. "I didnae expect it to be ye."

There was warmth in his gaze. "I needed to assure myself that ye did indeed agree to marry me. I pray it wasn't just a wonderful dream."

Without hesitation, she walked to him and leaned into his chest. "I will be yer wife." Lifting her face, to his soft kiss, embers of warmth came to life in her stomach.

"Why are ye nae wearing yer arm sling?"

"The healer wished for me to keep my arm still so that the stitches held. Not one is torn, so I am confident it is nae needed."

Fiery heat burned her cheeks, and Sencha covered them with her hands.

Knox took her hands and kissed each cheek. "I love how ye face brightens."

"I dinnae. Everyone will ken something happened between us."

With a shrug, he replied, "What they will think is that ye are excited and happy." He pressed a light kiss to her lips. "Today, we must speak to Alexander and Nala. Then to yer mother before making our betrothal public."

This time the heat was that of joy and Sencha couldn't keep from smiling.

CHAPTER NINETEEN

"**W**HERE DO YE wish to have the wedding ceremony?" her mother asked, her voice brimming with excitement, her cheeks flushed with joy. "The chapel at the keep is lovely this time of year."

Sencha exchanged a glance with Knox, who smiled faintly, his calm demeanor a stark contrast to the whirlwind of questions they'd been fielding since announcing their betrothal. Most answers had been variations of the same, *"We've not discussed it yet,"* or *"We dinnae ken."*

Finally, her mother threw up her hands, a warm laugh escaping her lips. "Forgive me for pestering ye with so many questions. I'm just so happy for ye both. It's understandable ye've yet to settle on the details."

Knox reached for Sencha's hand under the table, giving it a reassuring squeeze. Somehow, his steady presence kept her grounded while her own nerves were frayed by the sheer number of decisions looming before them.

"While I cook the meal, why do ye nae go for a wee walk?" her mother suggested, her eyes twinkling. "Clear yer heads and enjoy some time together."

The crisp air outside greeted them as they stepped into the fading light of late afternoon. Sencha pulled her cloak tightly around her, though the chill was barely noticeable. Excitement warmed her far more than her woolen layers. Excitement for the handsome man walking beside her who was soon to be her husband.

As they strolled through the woodlands, Knox glanced at her, his hazel eyes soft. "I will begin with the question both Alex and yer parents asked," he said. "Where do ye wish to live after we marry?"

Sencha thought for a moment, stepping over a small branch that had fallen in their path. "Since ye will continue to serve the laird, I think it makes sense to remain at the keep. Perhaps in a pair of years, once we have bairns, we can discuss building a house of our own."

Knox nodded, a thoughtful expression crossing his face. "I agree. My own lands are midway between yer current home and the keep," he added, gesturing in a direction that made sense. "Far enough inland to avoid the coastal winds, but close enough to either place."

She smiled, content with the practicality of their plans. But as they continued walking, Knox suddenly stopped and turned to face her. Before she could question him he stepped closer, cupping her face in his large hands, his touch warm against her chilled cheeks. Without hesitation, he captured her lips in a kiss that left her breathless, his mouth moving over hers with a passion that stole her thoughts.

When they finally broke apart, he gazed down at her, his lips curving into a crooked smile. "I will never tire of the taste of ye."

Sencha laughed softly, though her face burned with heat. "Knox," she teased, swatting lightly at his arm. "We've decisions to make. This is nae time for flattery."

"Flattery is it?" he murmured, leaning down as if to kiss her again. But she stepped back with a grin, steering the conversation back to practical matters.

"Should we marry at the keep or in the village?" she asked.

Knox rubbed his jaw, his brow furrowing slightly. "I think I prefer the keep. Something intimate, with only yer family and mine."

"I agree," Sencha said. "I will insist to Nala that she nae invite the entire clan."

They laughed, their voices mingling in the stillness of the woods, and resumed their walk. They talked about which chambers they would occupy at the keep, how many children they hoped to have, and the nature of Knox's duties. But as they neared her home again, Sencha's heart grew heavy with unspoken thoughts.

Knox must have noticed her distraction. His sharp eyes darted toward her, his expression shifting. "Something bothers ye," he said. "What is it?"

She hesitated, then blurted, "I must ask about other women." Her cheeks flamed, but she pressed on. "I cannae marry ye if ye plan to keep lovers."

Knox stopped, his brows lifting in surprise. Taking her by the shoulders, he turned her to face him fully. "Sencha," he said firmly, his voice rich with sincerity. "I give ye my solemn oath never to stray. The tales of my 'prowess' are greatly exaggerated. But I will nae lie to ye. I was involved with a woman until just before we hunted for yer dog."

Her breath caught, but she remained silent, watching him closely.

"I was about to be with her that day," he admitted, his

voice lowering, "but ye stumbled upon... Well, ye ken the rest." He exhaled deeply, his hands sliding down her arms. "I've nae sought anyone since that day. Ye have my word."

Sencha studied him, her gaze unwavering. "I thought there was something odd about yer horse being tethered so far from where ye were. Was it Anni?"

Knox shook his head. "Nae, someone else. I've never been with her."

Her jaw tightened, but her voice was steady. "I trust ye to ensure this woman is told never to approach ye again."

There was a stern finality in her tone, and Knox nodded solemnly. "It will be done as ye ask. I fear for anyone who betrays ye."

Sencha giggled, the tension easing as she smiled up at him. "I cannae think of anything else to discuss."

"There's the matter of our wedding date," Knox said, his tone lightening. He nudged her playfully with his shoulder. "I dinnae wish to wait long."

"Neither do I," Sencha replied, laughter dancing in her voice as they turned toward her home.

HENDRY RODE STEADILY along the well-worn road with five of his men, the clatter of hooves mingling with the occasional rustle of bare branches swaying in the wind. The chill of the late day bit into their faces, their breaths misting in the icy air. Weary from a long day of patrol, their expressions were grim and set, their shoulders hunched beneath their cloaks. The promise of the warm hearth and hearty meal waiting in the great hall of the keep was the only thing driving them forward.

As they neared the fork in the road that led to Ailith's small cottage, Hendry found his thoughts drifting to the widow. She lived alone, beyond the main routes patrolled by the laird's guards. It wasn't part of his direct responsibility, but the thought of her isolated and vulnerable gnawed at him. He doubted anyone had stopped by to check on her recently. She wasn't the sort to invite company, and her prickly demeanor kept most people at bay.

Hendry slowed his horse and raised a hand, signaling the others to halt. The men reined in their mounts, casting curious glances his way. "I will go to see about someone," he said, his tone leaving no room for argument. "Continue to the keep. I shall be there shortly."

None of the men protested. They were too eager to escape the cold and find warmth at the keep to offer to stay. With curt nods, they spurred their horses forward, their figures soon swallowed by the shadowy trees lining the road.

Turning his mount toward the woods, Hendry guided the animal along the narrow path leading to Ailith's home. The dense trees offered some reprieve from the biting wind, their skeletal branches creaking softly overhead.

As he emerged from the trees, the small cottage came into view, nestled in a clearing. A thin trail of smoke spiraled up from the chimney, a sign that Ailith was home and keeping the cold at bay. He dismounted with a practiced ease, his boots crunching against the leaf laden ground. Leaving his horse to graze, he approached the door and knocked twice, the sound echoing in the stillness.

From inside came the sharp bark of Teller, the shaggy dog

she called her own. Hendry waited, adjusting his cloak against the chill, until the door creaked open just enough to reveal Ailith's face. She scowled at him, her dark eyes narrowing suspiciously.

"Ye may as well enter, else the air will cool my house," she said tartly, pulling the door wider but still managing to look displeased. "There is nae a need for ye to come here."

Her dog bounded forward, sniffing his leg with enthusiasm. After a moment, Teller's tail wagged in recognition, but Ailith snapped her fingers sharply. The dog obeyed, retreating to the hearth and curling up. Though his watchful eyes remained fixed on Hendry.

Stepping inside, Hendry's presence filled the small room as the door closed behind him. The warmth of the fire greeted him, a stark contrast to Ailith's frosty demeanor. She crossed her arms, clearly unamused by the intrusion.

Apparently, whatever gratitude she might have felt when he'd helped her during her illness had vanished. She'd returned to her usual sharp dislike, her expression as cold as the air outside. Hendry brushed off her scowl, his gaze sweeping the room. The fire crackled in the hearth, and a pot hung above it, likely simmering some simple fare. The furnishings were modest and well-worn, the evidence of a life lived with little to spare.

"Will ye require chopped wood for the winter?" he asked, his voice steady and businesslike. "Is yer roof in good repair?"

She opened her mouth to reply, but he continued before she could speak. "If ye need blankets or food, the laird's wife would like ye to ken they will be brought to ye."

Ailith's lips pressed into a tight line, her annoyance evident as she stared at him. She shifted her weight, looking as though she was debating whether to throw him out or respond. Hendry remained calm, waiting, his hands hanging loosely at his sides.

Her gaze flickered to the neatly stacked pile of wood by the hearth before drifting upward to the ceiling, her lips pressing into a thin line. After a moment, she shook her head and squared her shoulders. "I dinnae require anything from ye, the laird, or his wife," she said, her voice firm and tinged with quiet anger. "What I need, I will ask my family to help with."

Hendry studied her. He knew all too well the truth of her situation. The only family she had was her sister, married with a brood of four or five bairns underfoot. From what little he'd seen of them, they were a struggling lot themselves, barely scraping by. The notion that they could spare anything for Ailith seemed unlikely at best.

Her own means were meager—midwifery and selling herbs she foraged from the woods at the village square. A coin here. A coin there, Just enough to scrape by. Likely, it was all spent on food, with nothing left for comforts or repairs. The threadbare clothes she wore, washed thin by time and toil, spoke of winters endured without proper warmth.

Hendry's gaze swept the room again, taking in the shabby state of the cottage. He could picture the drafts sneaking in through gaps in the walls and around the doorframe, stealing what little heat the fire offered.

He ignored her words and moved toward the hearth, his boots scuffing softly against the uneven floorboards. He crouched down and inspected the woodpile more closely, his frown deepening. "Is this all yer wood?" he asked, his tone neutral.

Ailith folded her arms across her chest and pressed her lips together in defiant silence.

Straightening, Hendry turned his attention to the ceiling. The patches of light filtering through the thatch confirmed his earlier observation. Two places were nearly bare and sure to leak with the next rain. His gaze dropped to a chair by the hearth, where a blanket was draped. It was thick enough for now, but its frayed edges and worn fabric told him it might not last another season. He imagined her huddled beneath it during the long, bitter nights of winter, the wind howling through the cracks.

"I'll patch the roof and chop some wood," he announced evenly, his voice carrying a note of finality.

Ailith stiffened, her face hardening as anger flared in her eyes. "I dinnae want any help from the people who allowed my husband to die," she snapped. "He didnae have to die."

Hendry's jaw tightened, but his voice remained calm. "No one should have to die," he said, meeting her gaze without flinching. "Neither Brant nor any of the others who lost their lives in battle."

Her lips parted, but instead of responding, she turned sharply on her heel and stalked to the door. She yanked it open with a jerk, and the icy wind rushed into the cottage, swirling around them like an unwelcome guest. "Leave," she demanded, her voice low but unyielding.

For a moment, Hendry didn't move. The cold air bit at his face, but he held her gaze, searching for something in her expression. Then, without a word, he strode past her, his heavy footfalls echoing in the small space. He stepped out into the chill, the door swinging shut behind him with a sharp finality.

Once outside, Hendry scanned the area and spotted a ladder leaning against the side of the house. Determined to help, he hefted it into place and climbed onto the roof. The cold air whipped around him as he crouched low, carefully inspecting the weathered thatch. He found two spots where the rain had seeped through, leaving gaps that desperately needed repair.

Climbing back down, he made his way to the woods nearby. The earthy scent of damp leaves and fresh pine filled the air as he gathered enough leafy branches to use as a temporary patch. His arms soon ached from the weight of the bundle, but he pressed on, knowing the effort would be worth it. Returning to the roof, Hendry worked with quiet focus, weaving the thin branches into the existing thatch. The job required several trips up and down the ladder, each climb testing his endurance. By the time he finished, the roof had a patchwork look, but it was sturdy enough to keep out the rain. He leaned back on his heels and surveyed his handiwork, nodding in satisfaction.

The next task waited for him below. A proper woodpile was essential, but when he searched for an ax, he came up empty-handed. It seemed the widow kept it inside the house, and he wasn't about to go knocking on her door. Undeterred, Hendry set out to collect fallen branches from the nearby woods. Armful by armful, he hauled them back to the cottage, stacking them neatly by the front door. The pile wasn't large, but it was enough to last several days. Long enough for him to hire someone to make more permanent repairs to the roof and tend to the firewood.

By the time he mounted his horse, the sun had begun its

slow descent, casting long shadows across the road. Despite the weariness he'd felt earlier, the physical labor had left him invigorated, his body buzzing with a sense of purpose. As he rode, his thoughts turned to the widow and what more he could do to ease her burden. Blankets, fabric, and food came to mind. Practical things she might need. He decided he'd arrange for everything to be delivered discreetly from the village, ensuring he'd avoid another clash with her sharp tongue.

The thought of her reaction—her annoyance, perhaps even her outrage at his meddling—made a crooked grin spread across his face. Before he knew it, Hendry was whistling a cheerful tune, the melody rising into the chilled evening air as he rode toward home.

EPILOGUE

T O SENCHA, THE four weeks they had waited to marry felt like an eternity. Each sunrise brought with it a flutter of anticipation, and each sunset a sigh of longing. Time seemed to stretch endlessly, every moment without Knox was much too long.

At long last, the day had arrived. The keep's chapel had been adorned with garlands of wildflowers, their delicate petals filling the air with a sweet, earthy fragrance. Soft candlelight bathed the stone walls in a warm glow as she and Knox exchanged vows, their voices steady yet filled with emotion. The ancient words bound them together, witnessed by those closest to them.

Now they sat side by side at the high table in the grand hall, guests of honor at the feast celebrating their union. The hall was alive with merriment—the clinking of tankards, bursts of laughter, and the lively strains of fiddles and pipes weaving through the air.

Sencha felt a radiant joy welling up inside her, so intense it threatened to overflow. Her gaze swept over the assembled guests, taking in each beloved face.

Her mother sat with Gordon, their eyes shining with pride and happiness. The lines of worry that had etched her mother's face for so long seemed smoothed away, replaced by a serene contentment.

Sencha turned her gaze to Knox who sat beside her, and her breath caught. He was breathtaking. Clad in the vibrant tartan of the Ross clan, his kilt draped elegantly over his strong frame. The crisp white of his tunic contrasted sharply with his tanned skin. His freshly shorn hair accentuated the chiseled lines of his face. His eyes, deep and clear, held a spark that sent a thrill through her. The heat radiating from his body was a comforting presence next to her, a silent promise of the warmth they would share in the nights to come. At a delightful shiver of anticipation, her cheeks flushed at the thought.

A group of guardsmen approached the table, their rugged faces softened by genuine smiles. Knox rose to greet them, clasping forearms and exchanging hearty embraces.

The hardened warriors, men accustomed to the stern demands of duty, became almost bashful in her presence. Each one offered her kind words and blessings, their voices gentler than she had ever heard them. They wished her and Knox every happiness, their eyes reflecting sincerity. She thanked them graciously, her heart swelling with gratitude for the camaraderie they shared with her husband—and now, with her.

The music in the hall swelled, filling every corner with its joyful melodies. Guests moved to the open space to dance, their movements spirited and unrestrained. Sencha's attention was drawn to a group of young women. They joined hands and spun in circles, skirts swirling around their ankles. She noticed the way their eyes darted toward the young men nearby. Furtive glances filled with hope and excitement. The men, attempting to appear aloof, couldn't hide the amused smiles tugging at their lips or the appreciative glances they cast in return.

"It was nae that long ago that it was us," Nala mused, her gaze on the dancers.

Sencha turned to her, a playful glint in her eye. "Ye never sought men's attention when ye were younger," she teased. "And from what ye've told me, that hasn't changed much."

Nala laughed softly, the sound like a gentle melody. "Perhaps not," she conceded, "but I always cherished the dancing and the freedom of those days."

Her laughter caught the ear of the laird. He looked over, his stern features softening as his eyes rested on his wife. "I enjoy dancing with ye now."

Nala's cheeks flushed ever so slightly, a tender smile curving her lips. "And I with ye," she replied softly, their exchange filled with unspoken affection.

Nala turned her attention back to Sencha. "When do ye think ye fell in love with Knox?" she asked gently, her eyes searching her friend's face.

Sencha leaned back, her thoughts drifting as she considered the question. "In truth, I cannae say for certain," she admitted. "Perhaps I've loved him for a very long time, without even realizing it. But the moment I allowed myself to acknowledge it, there was no turning back. It was as if a door had opened, and I could nae deny what was in my heart."

Just then, as if he sensed her thoughts, Knox turned away from his conversation with the guardsmen. His eyes found hers, and the bustling hall seemed to fade away. In his gaze, she saw a reflection of her own feelings. The depth of their love. The promise of a shared future. And the unspoken understanding that bound them together. A slow, tender smile curved his lips, and Sencha felt warmth spread through her entire being.

A man approached Knox and said something that made her husband animated, as he spoke his hands made gestures in the air.

With a broad grin, Knox leaned toward her and pressed a kiss to her lips. "My horse has returned. Do ye mind? I must go see him."

Happiness threatened to overspill, and tears filled Sencha's eyes. "Aye, go," she urged her heart leaping with joy.

Pulling her into a tight embrace her new husband's lips linger at her ear. "Be prepared to retire upon my return. Our wedding night has only just begun."

With a wicked grin, he met her gaze.

In that singular moment, surrounded by the joyous celebration of their marriage, Sencha knew with unwavering certainty that no stronger love could ever exist for her.

The world around them was vibrant and full of life, yet all she could see was Knox. The man who had captured her heart so completely. She returned his smile, her eyes shining with tears of happiness. Whatever challenges lay ahead, she knew they would face them together, their hearts forever entwined.

ABOUT THE AUTHOR

Enticing. Engaging. Romance.

USA Today Bestselling Author Hildie McQueen writes strong brooding alpha Highlanders who meet their match in feisty brave heroines. If you like stories with a mixture of passion, action, drama and humor, you will love Hildie's storytelling where love wins every single time!

A fan of all things pink, travel, and stationery, Hildie resides in eastern Georgia, USA, with her super-hero husband Kurt and three little yappy dogs.

Let's stay in touch, join my NEWSLETTER for free reads, previews of upcoming releases and news about my world!

www.ingramcontent.com/pod-product-compliance
Lightning Source LLC
Chambersburg PA
CBHW051953220626
47052CB00004B/932